'I had a very different plan in mind for you this evening.'

She sprang up, eyeing him in suspicion. 'Plan?'

'Turn of phrase, nothing more,' he said, taken aback. 'I just wanted to spend time getting to know you better.'

With a session in bed at the end of it? Sarah's chin lifted. 'I think I will go home now, please.'

Jake rose to his feet frowning. 'Why so soon? If I swear not to lay a finger on you, Sarah, will you stay for a while?'

She shook her head, refusing to meet his eyes.

D0997769

Imagine…

a picturesque spa town and pretty villages
that nestle deep in the heart of England…

Pennington Country…
In Pennington, the streets are filled with old-fashioned
buildings, quaint tearooms and irresistible shops…

In the surrounding villages, elegant manor houses
rub shoulders with cosy mellow stone cottages, and
everybody's gardens are ablaze with flowers…

Pennington Country…
Where the people are warm and charming,
and falling in love brings with it tender flirtations
and enchanting affairs…

Why not visit Catherine George's magical world
yourself in twelve other delightful stories?

Pennington titles by the same author:

SARAH'S SECRET

BY
CATHERINE GEORGE

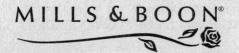

MILLS & BOON®

DID YOU PURCHASE THIS BOOK WITHOUT A COVER?

If you did, you should be aware it is **stolen property** as it was reported *unsold and destroyed* by a retailer. Neither the author nor the publisher has received any payment for this book.

All the characters in this book have no existence outside the imagination of the author, and have no relation whatsoever to anyone bearing the same name or names. They are not even distantly inspired by any individual known or unknown to the author, and all the incidents are pure invention.

All Rights Reserved including the right of reproduction in whole or in part in any form. This edition is published by arrangement with Harlequin Enterprises II B.V. The text of this publication or any part thereof may not be reproduced or transmitted in any form or by any means, electronic or mechanical, including photocopying, recording, storage in an information retrieval system, or otherwise, without the written permission of the publisher.

This book is sold subject to the condition that it shall not, by way of trade or otherwise, be lent, resold, hired out or otherwise circulated without the prior consent of the publisher in any form of binding or cover other than that in which it is published and without a similar condition including this condition being imposed on the subsequent purchaser.

MILLS & BOON and MILLS & BOON with the Rose Device are registered trademarks of the publisher.

*First published in Great Britain 2002
Harlequin Mills & Boon Limited,
Eton House, 18-24 Paradise Road, Richmond, Surrey TW9 1SR*

© Catherine George 2002

ISBN 0 263 82970 7

*Set in Times Roman 10½ on 12 pt.
01-1002-47587*

*Printed and bound in Spain
by Litografía Rosés, S.A., Barcelona*

CHAPTER ONE

THE sky was ominous with the threat of approaching storm, but Sarah finally gave up trying to find a taxi during Friday rush hour and began hurrying at top speed through the dark, sultry afternoon. Hot and breathless, she was almost in sight of home when a curtain of rain poured from the heavens as though someone had thrown a switch. Lightning sizzled to earth almost at her feet, thunder cracked directly overhead, and with a scream she raced, panicking, through the alley that led to Campden Road. Drenched to the skin, she shot from the alley like a cork from a bottle and flew across the road through the downpour, straight into the path of a car. With a squeal of brakes the car slewed sharply to avoid her, but the front wing of the car caught her a light, glancing blow which sent her sprawling on hands and knees. Shaken and furious, she scrambled to her feet, shrugging off urgent hands which hauled her back on the pavement.

'Are you all right? Where the *hell* did you spring from?' yelled the stranger above another clap of thunder.

'Of course I'm not all right, you stupid idiot!' She glared up at a wet male face haggard with shock. 'Can't you look where you're going?'

'I *was* looking,' he flung at her. 'For which you can thank your lucky stars, lady. If my reactions had been slower things could have been a sight worse. You came out of nowhere!'

'I did *not*. I was just crossing the road.'

5

'You mean you shot across without looking.'

'Look here, *I'm* the injured party,' she retorted furiously, then bit back a scream, her teeth chattering as lightning forked down again close by, followed by another crack of thunder.

The man seized her arm. 'You're in shock. And soaked to the skin. Get in the car. I'll drive you to the hospital—'

'The way *you* drive? Not a chance!' Sarah pulled free so viciously her head swam as she bent to retrieve her scattered belongings, and the man caught her by the shoulders to hold her steady for a moment before bending to help her. Their heads banged together, she recoiled with a yelp, and with a muttered apology he handed over a bunch of keys, frowning when she winced as she took them.

'You *are* hurt.' He seized one of her hands, where the rain was sluicing grit and blood from a scrape, but Sarah snatched it away, horribly conscious, now, of hair dripping round her face in rats' tails, and blouse soaked to a transparency the man had obviously noticed. Colour flooded her face.

'It's only a scratch. I'll live,' she snapped. 'Which is no thanks to you.'

'If you won't go to a hospital at least let me drive you home.'

'*No.* I am home. I live over there,' she shouted as thunder boomed around them.

'Then I'll get you there in one piece.' Ignoring her protests, he took her briefcase, grasped her by the elbow and hurried her across the road through the sheeting rain.

'I should take you to a hospital,' he insisted, but Sarah shook her head, refusing to meet his eyes as he handed over the briefcase.

'Unnecessary.'

'Is there someone inside to take care of you?'

'Yes, there is. You can go now.' Sarah unlocked the front door of one of the tall Victorian houses lining the road, muttered a word of ungracious thanks, went inside, and slammed the door. She dumped her bags down in the gloomy hall, knees trembling as reaction hit her, but unmoved now when thunder cracked overhead. She was safe.

'Good heavens, just look at you,' said her grandmother, hurrying downstairs. 'You're soaked to the skin.' She frowned as she saw Sarah's knees. 'What happened? Did you fall?'

Sarah made light of her wounds and went to the bathroom to get her sodden clothes off. She mopped at her grazes, then returned to the kitchen, wrapped in a towelling dressing gown. She sat down at the table, surprised but grateful to find tea waiting for her, and rubbed at her wet hair with a sleeve while she gave an account of her adventure.

'You should go to the police!' said Margaret Parker severely. 'You could have been badly injured. I suppose it was the usual boy racer taking a shortcut to the town centre?'

'Not this time. It was a *very* angry adult of the species, who insisted I was to blame.'

'And were you?'

'Certainly not!' Sarah met her grandmother's eyes, then shrugged. 'Well, yes, I suppose I was, really. I was in my usual panic, so I didn't look properly before crossing the road.'

'You really must try to control your irrational fear of storms, you know.'

'Not entirely irrational,' said Sarah quietly.

Margaret Parker backed down at once. 'Was the man objectionable?'

'Not exactly. But he was steamingly angry. Once he knew I was in one piece he obviously wanted to shake the living daylights out of me.'

'Typical male! What sort of age was he?'

'No idea. We were both soaked to the skin, and I didn't have my contacts in, so one way and another my powers of observation were on the blink.' Sarah eyed the rain streaming down the window. 'Good thing I don't have to drive through this to collect Davy today.'

'But you're going to the theatre tonight,' Margaret reminded her.

'Heavens, so I am.' Sarah groaned, then shook her head wearily. 'I just can't face it tonight, peeved though Brian will be. If I ring him now I'll catch him before he leaves the office.'

'Surely you'll feel better by this evening?' said her grandmother disapprovingly. 'Brian won't be happy if you let him down at the last minute.'

'I'm sure he'll understand if I explain.' Sarah heaved herself up from the table to peer through the window. 'The storm's moving away a bit, so I think I'll soak my wounds in a hot bath. I feel a bit shivery.'

'Reaction. It will soon wear off. Was the man hurt, by the way?'

'No idea. But serve him right if he was!'

Margaret raised an eyebrow. 'I thought you were to blame?'

'I was.' Sarah smiled wryly. 'Which is so *aggravating*. I want someone else to blame. Preferably him.'

When Sarah rang Brian Collins his reaction was just as predicted.

'Sarah, you do realise that I had the devil of a job to

get tickets?' he demanded irritably, then climbed down a little. 'Though I'm sorry you're feeling unwell, of course.'

'And I'm sorry to cancel at the last minute. But there must be someone else you can take, Brian?'

He was silent for a moment. 'Since Davina's not there for once I could just return the tickets and spend the evening at home with you.'

Sarah blenched. '*No*—no, don't do that, Brian. I'd hate you to miss the play on my account. I know you were looking forward to it.'

'Very well, then,' he said, resigned. 'I'll ring you next week.'

Sarah rang off, her eyes thoughtful. Her association with Brian Collins, undemanding in most ways though it was, had definitely run its course. He was a nice, conventional man, pleasant enough company for an occasional evening out, but there were two major drawbacks to their relationship. One was an ongoing argument due to Sarah's refusal to become physically involved. The other was that in theory Brian felt he should get on with children, but in practice found it so difficult Davy couldn't stand him.

Not, thought Sarah, as she lay in a blissfully hot bath later, that Brian sees very much of her. Nor can I let Davy rule my life for ever. One day she'll be up and away and I'll be free to do as I like. Chilled by the idea of Davy grown up and independent, Sarah pulled the bathplug and concentrated on the episode in the storm instead. But, hard as she tried to bring her rescuer's face into focus, it remained a dark, rainwashed blur. He'd been a lot taller than her, and strong, by the way he'd manhandled her. But otherwise she had only a general impression of broad shoulders outlined by a soaked white shirt, dark hair and eyes, and a face so haggard with shock that if she met him again in the street she probably wouldn't recognise him. Which, all things considered, was probably just as well.

By the time Sarah was dressed the sky was clear, and she began to relax at last. And, though it was strange to be without Davy on a Friday evening, she wasn't sorry to have this particular one to herself after her scary little adventure.

On her way out for her bridge evening Margaret Parker came down from her apartment upstairs to hand over a supermarket bag. 'I forgot this in all the excitement—the shopping I did for you this morning.'

Sarah thanked her, handed over the money, then groaned as the buzzer sounded on the outer door. 'I hope that's not Brian on a flying visit before the theatre.'

'Sarah, really!' remonstrated her grandmother.

But when Sarah spoke into her receiver she found it was a florist's delivery. 'Are you sure it's for Tracy?' she asked, surprised.

'No name, just the number of the house,' said the disembodied voice.

Sarah hurried to open the front door, taken aback when she was handed an enormous bouquet of fragrant lilies.

'How thoughtful,' said her grandmother in approval. 'Brian, of course?'

'Actually no,' said Sarah, not without satisfaction, and handed over a card which read, *'With sincere apologies, J. Hogan.'*

'A courteous gesture,' conceded Margaret reluctantly.

Sarah shrugged. 'Just salving his conscience.' She thought for a moment. 'Hogan. The name's familiar. I wonder if he's on our firm's database?'

'Did he look familiar?'

'Couldn't tell. I doubt if I'd even know him again.'

Later, taking pleasure in having the entire house to herself, Sarah made herself some supper and settled down to enjoy it on the sofa in her sitting room, with the glass doors open to the garden at the back of the house.

'Nice move,' she told the striking arrangement of lilies.

During the evening a very excited Davina rang up to ask if they were doing anything special the next day.

'No, darling. Why?' asked Sarah.

'Because Polly's mummy says can I go bowling with them tomorrow and stay the night again? Can I? *Please?* Here's Mrs Rogers,' she added, before Sarah, astonished, could say another word.

Alison Rogers gave assurances that they would be delighted to keep Davy for another day. Sarah expressed grateful, rather bemused thanks, and, after a few instructions on behaviour to an ecstatic Davy, arranged to collect her on Sunday instead of the next day.

Sarah's feelings were mixed when she returned to her book. It was the first time Davy had spent a night away from her, apart from school, and the child was obviously having such a good time with Polly she was even happy to skip part of her weekend at home. Suppressing a wry little pang at the thought, Sarah felt pleased that Davy was beginning to spread her wings at last. At nearly nine years old Davina Tracy was tall for her age, but an endearing mixture of maturity and little-girl dependence. To want to spend her precious weekend away from Sarah was a first in Davy Tracy's young life.

Next morning Sarah felt no ill effects after her adventure in the storm, other than the discovery that Mr J.

Hogan's car had left a spectacular bruise on her thigh. Hoping she'd left a corresponding dent somewhere on its chassis, she went off to load the washing machine, then took her breakfast out to the table in the sunlit courtyard outside the sitting room windows. Sarah went through the Saturday morning paper while she ate, and had read it from cover to cover by the time her grandmother came outside in her gardening clothes.

'You look fully recovered this morning, Sarah,' Margaret commented.

'I'm fine now. It seems funny without Davy on a Saturday morning, but I did enjoy the extra hour in bed. And I've read all my favourite bits of the paper in one go for once. By the way,' Sarah added, pulling up the leg of her shorts, 'take a look. My souvenir of yesterday's adventure.'

'Does it hurt?'

'Only if I bump into something.' Sarah stretched luxuriously. 'It's a lovely day. Once I've hung out my laundry I'm off into town for some shopping. Can I fetch you anything?'

Sarah's Saturdays were always given over to Davy. And, much as she looked forward to spending them with her child, it was a pleasant change to be on her own for once, free to browse as long as she liked in the numerous bookshops in the town. After treating herself to a cut-price bestseller she made a preliminary foray through the summer sale in the town's largest department store, then went up to the coffee shop on the top floor. While she enjoyed a peaceful sandwich Sarah couldn't help comparing it with the pizza Davy invariably clamoured for, and hoped her child was enjoying something similar with the Rogers family.

Sarah lingered over coffee afterwards, looking down

on a view of the Parade through the trees, and afterwards went down a couple of floors to find a dress in the sale. With regret she dismissed a rail of low-cut strappy little numbers. As usual, her aim was a dress for all seasons: office, prize day at school, even the odd evening out.

Eventually, after checking the price tags of every possibility in her size, Sarah found a dress in clinging almond-pink jersey. It draped slightly, sported a minor designer label, and displayed exactly the right length of long, suntanned leg she was rather vain about. She examined herself critically, checked on her back view, and decided she could do no better with the money she could afford.

When she got home Sarah went up to her grandmother's flat to hand over the vitamin pills Margaret had asked her to buy, showed her the dress, then reported that she was off to read in the garden for a while before getting on with her homework.

Sarah went out with her new book to lie on an old steamer chair under an umbrella for a while, a brief interlude which did nothing at all, later, for her enthusiasm for the work she always brought home with her. Her job entailed a nine-to-three working day for a specialist recruitment firm, where she dealt with client liaison, database management, and the most urgent of the daily correspondence. The bulk of the latter she took home with her, to finish on a computer supplied by the firm for the purpose. It was an arrangement that suited both Sarah and her employers, and she was well aware that the job was as ideal as she was ever likely to find in her circumstances. The salary was generous for part-time work, and the hours were convenient for someone with a child. Her grandmother shared some of the responsibility for Davy, but Margaret Parker was an active member of her church, played bridge regularly, and served on the committees of several high-profile charities. She led such a busy social life Sarah asked her to look after Davy only in emergencies.

Later that evening, when Margaret Parker had gone off to the theatre with a friend, to see the play her granddaughter had missed out on, the doorbell rang just as Sarah was switching off the computer.

'Ms Tracy?' said a man's voice through the intercom. 'My name's Hogan. Could you spare a moment to talk to me, please?'

Her eyebrows rose. What on earth did *he* want? But, eager to find out, Sarah asked him to wait a moment, exchanged her glasses for contact lenses, did some lightning work with a lipstick and hairbrush, then opened the front door to confront a tall man dressed in jeans and a plain white shirt. Now it was dry his hair wasn't black but dark blond, tipped with gold at the ends. And the eyes she'd thought dark were the ultramarine blue of one of Davina's crayons. Sarah liked the look of him now she could see him clearly. And suddenly wished she were wearing something more appealing.

'I apologise for intruding on a Saturday night,' he said, after a silence spent in gazing at her with an intensity she found rather unnerving, 'but I wanted to make sure you came to no harm yesterday.'

Sarah hesitated, then opened the door wider. 'Please come in.' She led the way along the hall to the sitting room, opened the glass doors and took her visitor outside. She motioned him to one of the chairs at the garden table, and sat down.

'Thank you for seeing me,' he said at once, the blue eyes very direct. 'I was worried last night after you refused to let me take you to a hospital.'

'The fault was more mine than yours, Mr Hogan,' she admitted reluctantly. 'And thank you for the flowers. They're beautiful.'

'My olive branch.' He smiled a little. 'Actually, this is my second visit of the day. I came round to see you this morning, but you were out.'

Sarah smiled back, then on impulse offered him a drink.

A flash of surprise lit the striking, dark-lashed eyes. 'Are you sure I'm not keeping you from something?'

'Not a thing,' she admitted reluctantly, wishing she could say that some handsome escort was about to sweep her off to dine and dance the night away.

'Then thank you. I'd like that very much. It's thirsty weather.'

'I'm afraid it's just beer or a glass of wine.'

'A beer sounds wonderful.'

Sarah hurried off to fetch one of the cans kept for the man who helped in the garden, filled a stein which had once belonged to her father, then half-filled a glass for herself and topped it up with Davy's lemonade.

'Time I introduced myself properly,' said her visitor, rising to his feet when she got back. 'Jacob Hogan.'

'Sarah Tracy,' she responded with a smile, and sat down, waving him back to his chair.

'I kept thinking I should have insisted on taking you to the hospital yesterday,' he said ruefully. 'You were on my mind all evening.'

Sarah shrugged. 'You needn't have worried. My main problem was fright. Not just from the encounter with your car, either. I suffer from chronic cowardice in thunderstorms. Which is why I wasn't paying attention to the traffic.'

'Understandable.' He leaned back in the chair as he

sipped his beer, looking relaxed, as though he meant to stay for a while. Something Sarah, rather to her surprise, found she didn't object to in the slightest.

She looked at him questioningly. 'Your name's familiar. The Hogan part.'

'Tiles,' he said, resigned.

Sarah smiled. 'Oh, of course! Pentiles. We used them in the new bathroom. Imported, and *very* expensive.'

He shook his head. 'Not all our lines. We provide for all tastes and pockets.'

'I know. I read about your company in the local paper. Quite a success story.'

'Then you probably know my father started it off with just one hardware shop?'

She nodded. 'He obviously expanded big-time at some stage. Is it true that you now have retail outlets all over the country?'

'Pretty much. The whole thing took off at amazing speed when I finally persuaded Dad that ceramic tiles were the way forward.' He shrugged. 'These days people expect more than one bathroom—power showers, bigger kitchens, conservatories—all good for our line of business.'

'Is it entirely family-run?'

'The only Hogans in Pentiles are my father and myself. My brother's CV is more glamorous. Liam's an investment banker, and lives in London.' He smiled. 'I distribute tiles and live here in Pennington. I was making a detour through Campden Road to my place yesterday, trying to dodge rush hour traffic in the town centre.' His eyes gleamed. 'At which point you gave me the worst fright of my entire life.'

'I gave *you* a fright?' Sarah said indignantly. 'For a

moment my life flashed past before my eyes. I've got the scars to prove it, too.' She held out her grazed palms.

He leaned forward to inspect them, and for a wild moment Sarah thought he was going to kiss them better, but he sat back, giving her the straight blue look again.

'I apologise. Again. So, Miss Tracy. You know about my tiles. May I ask what you do with your life?'

Wishing it was more interesting, Sarah described her job briefly, then offered him another drink. And wished she hadn't when he took this as a signal to leave.

'I didn't mean to take up so much of your time,' he said, getting to his feet, then smiled warmly, his eyes crinkling at the corners. 'Thank you for seeing me. And for the beer.'

When Sarah led the way inside he paused, his attention caught by a photograph on a side table. On their one and only excursion as a threesome Brian, who prided himself on his skill with a camera, had snapped Sarah and Davy laughing together from their perch on a five-barred gate. The result was so happy Sarah had framed it. Bright sunshine gleamed on two heads of glossy nut-brown hair, and picked out gold flecks in identical brown eyes.

'She's yours, of course,' commented her visitor. 'The likeness is remarkable. How old is she?'

'Davina will be nine soon.'

'*Nine?*' His eyes were incredulous as he turned to look at her. 'You must have been very young when she was born!'

Sarah nodded. 'Eighteen.' She went ahead of him along the hall to open the front door, and held out her hand to her unexpected guest. 'It was very kind of you to come round, Mr Hogan. And I assure you that my dignity was the worst casualty during our encounter. Not counting my temper,' she added ruefully. 'I'm sorry I screamed at you like a fishwife.'

'Hardly surprising—you'd had a hell of a shock. I was shattered myself.' He took her hand very carefully for a moment, mindful of the grazes, and gave her a look she couldn't interpret. 'I hope your wounds heal soon, Mrs Tracy.'

'Actually, it's *Miss* Tracy,' she corrected casually, and smiled. 'Thank you for coming, Mr Hogan.'

His sudden answering smile held a warmth Sarah responded to involuntarily. 'It was my pleasure—a great pleasure,' he assured her. 'And I answer to Jake.'

CHAPTER TWO

SARAH was reading when her grandmother called in to report on the play. Margaret Parker's eyebrows rose when she heard about the unexpected visitor.

'Hogan? I'm sure I've heard that name somewhere quite recently.'

'You probably read his success story in the local paper. He's the brains behind Pentiles.'

'The tiles we used in your bathroom? How impressive.'

'He called this morning, too, while I was out. You were probably in the garden and didn't hear the bell.' Sarah gave her grandmother a challenging little smile. 'Actually, I'm glad I was out. It meant I enjoyed a pleasant interlude in the garden with a very attractive stranger. Spiced up my Saturday evening no end.'

'You've changed your tune since last night,' said Margaret tartly. 'Although you should be grateful to this Mr Hogan for making you miss the play.' She looked down her nose. 'The ex-soap star may have drawn the crowds in, but Oscar Wilde was probably spinning in his Paris grave at her interpretation of Lady Windermere.'

'Oh, dear. You think Brian disapproved?'

'Her costumes displayed so much cleavage I'm sure the male half of the audience were *very* happy.'

Sarah chuckled. 'Brian's not that sort.'

Margaret's mouth tightened. 'All men are that sort. As you very well know.'

Sarah took a while to get to sleep that night, trying to

remember exactly what she'd read about Pentiles. She knew that Jacob Hogan had taken over the family business when quite young, and eventually turned it into its present success story. But to her annoyance she couldn't remember if a wife had been mentioned in the article.

She sighed despondently. Not that it mattered. Men tended to lose interest in her once they found she came as a package with Davy. One look at her child's photograph had probably killed all personal interest on Jake Hogan's part. Brian, to his credit, had insisted that Sarah's responsibilities as a single parent made no difference to their relationship. And in principle, she conceded, they probably hadn't. Not that this had ever worried Sarah much because she had known from the beginning that, no matter how much her grandmother stressed Brian's eligibility, there was no future in the relationship. Quite apart from the problem with Davy, he just didn't appeal to Sarah in the normal male-female way.

Jake Hogan, on the other hand, appealed to her a lot. In every way. A fright and a graze or two were a small price to pay for meeting the most attractive man to enter her life to date, even if it was just a one-off experience.

Next morning Sarah drove out of town for a couple of miles to make for the Rogers home, where screams of laughter could be heard coming from the depths of its vast, wild garden when she arrived. Alison Rogers welcomed her into the house and took her straight to a big, comfortably untidy kitchen, where it was pleasant to sit for a while and chat over coffee while Don Rogers went to collect Polly and Davina.

'Thank you so much for having Davy,' Sarah said gratefully. 'This was quite a big step for her. She's never wanted a sleepover before, let alone a whole extra day away from home.'

'She told me that,' said Alison, pleased. 'We're flattered. And as far as we're concerned Davy can make a return visit any time. It was far less trouble for us than keeping Polly entertained on her own. Now she's a weekly boarder our daughter demands our undivided attention every minute of the day at weekends. I expect it's the same with Davy.'

'Absolutely!'

'But you have to cope on your own, which must be hard.' Alison bit her lip. 'I'm sorry, Sarah. I didn't mean to get personal. But Davy told us she's never had a daddy.'

'That's right,' said Sarah cheerfully. 'Men don't feature in Davy's life, so I hope your husband didn't find her too much of a nuisance.'

'Don took to her on sight—as you can see.' Alison got up to point through the window, where her large husband was tearing towards the house in mock terror, with two little girls chasing after him, screaming in delight.

Sarah laughed as she watched Don Rogers capture a little girl under each arm and run with them into the house.

'Right,' he panted as he set them down. 'Which one would you like, Sarah?'

'Mummy!' Davy launched herself at Sarah to hug her, looking flushed and grubby and thoroughly pleased with herself. 'We went bowling and had pizzas and we talked *all* night.'

'Most of it, anyway,' said Alison indulgently.

'You've obviously had a marvellous time,' said Sarah, ruffling Davy's hair.

'Mummy says Davy can come *every* weekend,' said Polly hopefully.

Her father chuckled. 'We might like that, but I think Sarah would miss her.'

'How about coming to stay with Davy and me some time, instead, Polly?' suggested Sarah. 'Our garden's not as big as yours, but we could go swimming, and to the cinema, maybe.'

Polly clamoured at once for permission, a date was set for two weeks later, and Alison suggested Sarah drove Polly back afterwards. 'Join us for Sunday lunch that day. Davy too, of course. We'll invite some of the neighbours in, make it a party.'

Sarah made no attempt to hide her pleasure. This was the kind of invitation which never came her way. 'That's so kind of you, I'd love to.'

On the way home Davy chattered incessantly, giving Sarah every detail of her stay with Polly. 'Mr Rogers is lovely,' she said with enthusiasm. 'Mrs Rogers, too,' she added hastily, 'but she couldn't play with us all the time, because she had to do cooking and stuff.'

'A woman's lot,' said Sarah with a dramatic sigh, and Davy giggled.

'You don't cook *all* the time.'

'True. Grandma's making Sunday lunch at this very moment.'

'What are we having?' said Davy, eyes sparkling.

'I know about lots of vegetables, because I did them for her before I came out. And I'm sure Grandma's rustling up something yummy to go with them.'

When they hurried upstairs in Campden Road, delicious scents of roast chicken came wafting from Margaret's kitchen. She came down to meet them, smiling with a warmth she never showed Sarah as she opened her arms for Davy to fling herself into them and give a second account of her activities over the weekend.

'Goodness, what an exciting time you've had,' said Margaret fondly. 'Now, go and wash in my bathroom, Davina Tracy. Lunch is nearly ready.' She exchanged a look with Sarah as the little girl raced off. 'She obviously enjoyed herself.'

'She certainly did. But brace yourself, because we've got Polly on a return visit in a fortnight.' Sarah's lips twitched. 'You could always take off on holiday a few days sooner than scheduled.'

'Certainly not,' said Margaret briskly. 'I shall be here as usual. But the Rogers child will be your responsibility, Sarah, not mine.'

The rest of the day went by in a flash, with only time for the cake Margaret always made for Davy's tea before Sarah drove the child back to school. This was a task she never looked forward to, though it was easier these days, now Davy had made friends. During her first term Davy had hated going back to school on Sunday evenings, and had been so tearful the journey had been purgatory for Sarah.

Given her own choice of education Sarah would have kept Davy at home and sent her to a local day school. But Margaret Parker had contributed to the money Sarah's parents had put in trust for school fees at Davy's birth, and had made sure that when the time came the child was sent to Roedale. And if Sarah suspected that Margaret had chosen the school for its social cachet, rather than its excellent academic record, she kept her thoughts to herself.

So, although Anne and David Tracy had died on holiday when Davina was only five, Sarah had kept her promise and eventually sent the child as a weekly boarder to the girls' school Margaret Parker had persuaded them to choose. But Sarah had never imagined beforehand how painful it would be to part with Davy every term-time Sunday evening.

When Brian rang after the weekend, with a belated enquiry after Sarah's health, she agreed readily when he suggested they had dinner together the following evening, glad of the opportunity to tell him it was over between them.

Over dinner at Brian's favourite restaurant Sarah listened patiently while he gave her a detailed account of the play she'd missed.

'The actress who played Lady Windermere was particularly good,' he informed her. 'Beautiful creature.'

'So I've heard,' murmured Sarah absently, her mind on the kindest way to tell him it was over between them. In the end Brian gave up on her, openly relieved when she refused pudding and coffee. He walked her back to the car at such a pace she assumed he was in a hurry to get home, then sat silent for a moment, making no move to switch on the ignition.

'Sarah, there's something I need to tell you,' he informed her heavily.

Because he'd taken the exact words out of her mouth she eyed him in surprise. 'Talk away, then, Brian.'

'I'm sorry I was poor company tonight,' he began, staring through the windscreen. 'Because, well—oh, dammit, there's no easy way to say this.'

'Are you by any chance giving me the push, Brian?' asked Sarah unsteadily, desperate to laugh.

'I wouldn't have put it quite like that,' he protested, and shot a hunted look at her. 'Look, my dear, I hate to do this to you in your particular situation.'

She stiffened. 'My situation?'

'Don't be offended,' he implored her. 'I think you do a wonderful job as a single parent. But—well—the truth is, Sarah, I'm just not cut out to be a stepfather,' he added in a rush.

Since Sarah, in her wildest dreams, had never cast him in the role, she agreed readily. 'No, Brian, I don't think you are.'

'But I must be honest. That's not the only reason,' he went on doggedly, and took a deep breath. 'It's been obvious to me for some time that a physical relationship between us is never going to happen, Sarah. And, contrary to the impression I may give, I'm a pretty normal kind of man, with the usual male needs, you know.'

'Oh, Brian, of course you are,' said Sarah in remorse. 'I'm sorry I couldn't fulfil them for you. I never meant to hurt you.'

'I know that, my dear.' He patted her hand. 'So I'll be straight with you, Sarah. I've met someone else. Amanda's just joined the firm. I took her to the theatre when you cancelled, and we found we were—well—instantly compatible in that way. Highly compatible. In fact I spent most of the weekend with her. Something which was never possible with you, because of Davina. Amanda knows I'm with you tonight, of course,' he added. 'But she was very sporting about it.'

'Good for her,' managed Sarah, trying to get her head round the idea of Brian involved in a hot, passionate relationship.

'I hope this isn't too upsetting for you,' he said, tugging at his tie. 'I wouldn't hurt you for the world.'

Sarah took a deep, steadying breath. 'Brian, I'm not upset and I'm not hurt. Truly. In fact I'm very happy for you. Now, drive me home.'

When she got in Sarah went straight upstairs to break the news she knew very well would annoy Margaret Parker. 'Sorry to interrupt, Grandma, but I thought you should know right away that Brian doesn't want to see me any more.'

Margaret stared in horror. 'Why ever not?' Her eyes narrowed suspiciously. 'What did you do to offend him, you silly girl? Brian Collins is such a good catch. His father owns half of Pennington—'

'It's more a case of what I didn't do,' interrupted Sarah.

'I don't understand.'

Sarah met her grandmother's eyes squarely. 'Oh, I think you do. I know you dislike the word, but sex was to blame.'

Margaret stiffened. 'Then you have only yourself to blame. You, of all people, know what happens when a woman drops into a man's arms like a ripe plum!'

Sarah's eyes flashed coldly. 'You've got it all wrong, Grandma. *Lack* of sex was the problem. I never cared for Brian in that way. So he's found someone who does. And good luck to him.'

Margaret Parker's face was a study. 'I—I see. I apologise,' she added with difficulty.

'Apology accepted.' Sarah turned at the door for her parting shot. 'And to top it all Brian came clean and admitted he couldn't see himself as Davy's stepfather.'

Feeling liberated after the departure of Brian from her life, Sarah rushed home from work the next afternoon to sit out in the garden and make the most of the heat wave. Not bothering to cook, she ate salad, and left the firm's daily quota of mail until the evening, when it was cooler. Margaret Parker, in conciliatory mood after the misunderstanding over Brian, had added extra salad vegetables to the shopping she'd offered to undertake for Sarah, and never mentioned the subject again, adhering to the rule of non-interference kept to on both sides from the day Sarah had taken Davy to live in the house in Campden Road.

To achieve privacy and independence for both Sarah and herself, Margaret Parker had divided her home into two separate, self-contained apartments before they'd set up house together. Though she would have infinitely preferred a place of her own for herself and Davy, Sarah knew this wasn't practical, and never forgot that she was a lot better off than many in her situation as a single parent. She had the huge advantage of a low-rent home, a steady, if not lavish, income from her job, and the knowledge that Davy's education was financially secure at a reputable school. Even if it wasn't the school of Sarah's choice. And now Davy had started boarding Sarah enjoyed evenings out with friends made through her job—if she were honest, she enjoyed herself more with Esther and Maggie from the agency than dining out with Brian.

Although Sarah was happy enough with her life she was human enough to yearn sometimes for an extra dimension to it, a feeling which intensified the next morning, when she received a long-expected wedding invitation from Nick Morrell, her closest friend from college days. He enclosed a note, urging her to bring her current man with her and stay for the dance afterwards, and emphasised that the old crowd were all looking forward to seeing her again.

Sarah's own standing within their group had been unique from the first. She had been afraid beforehand that her fatherless baby would be a handicap where friendships were concerned. But to her surprise and gratitude Davy's existence had been accepted as part of life

by the kindred spirits met at university, both male and female. Nick Morrell had been one of the friends close enough
to invite home, to meet her parents and play with Davy,
and they had kept in close touch ever since. But now Nick
was acquiring a wife things would be a lot different.

Sarah mulled over the invitation as she walked to
work, very much aware that if she went to the wedding
she would be the only one of her group without a partner. Though even if they'd still been on that kind of
footing Brian wouldn't have served the purpose. Unless
they'd undergone a sea change lately, her crowd were a
flippant, wise-cracking bunch. Sober Brian, anything
but, just wouldn't have fitted in. But she had a new dress,
she reminded herself. And the wedding was mid-week,
so no problem with Davy. She was due some time off.
All she needed were some shoes and a place to stay
overnight. A wedding present was an essential expense
whether she went or not. She decided to book a room
right away at the hotel Nick had recommended. It could
always be cancelled if she changed her mind.

After an even busier day than usual Sarah was glad
to escape at last, and, hoisting her bulging briefcase, set
off through the crowds thronging the pavements in the
afternoon sunshine. Sarah rarely took the car into work
in summer, relying on her walk to and from the town
centre for her daily quota of exercise. She was hurrying
for home, her thoughts on tea in the garden, when a car
stopped a little way ahead and a familiar male figure
leaned out, formal in a dark suit.

'Hello, there. Can I give you a lift?' Jake Hogan
asked, smiling.

Oh, yes, please, thought Sarah, and returned the smile
warmly as he reached over to open the passenger door
for her. 'How nice of you. Though I shouldn't, really.'

'You don't accept lifts from strange men?'

'Never!' Her eyes danced. 'Though I really meant that the walk is my daily gesture at keeping fit.'

He cast a comprehensive glance at her as they left the busiest part of town behind. 'It won't affect you much to skip it for once. You were hurrying,' he added. 'Do you need to get home urgently?'

'Only for tea in the garden.'

'Pleasant prospect,' he sighed. 'I'm on my way to a meeting.'

'In this neighbourhood?' she said, surprised.

'No, not really.' When he pulled up in Campden Road he switched off the ignition and turned to give her the smile she'd been thinking of rather a lot since the previous Saturday. 'Actually, my meeting's in town. But I spotted you hurrying down the street, so I did a quick U-turn to drive you home.'

Sarah felt a rush of secret pleasure. 'I might not have been going home,' she pointed out.

'In which case I would have driven you wherever you wanted to go.' His eyes crinkled. 'Or you could have refused politely and waved me on before I got nicked for kerb-crawling.'

Sarah laughed. 'I was very grateful for the ride. And now I'll let you get to your meeting,' she added, undoing the seatbelt.

'Don't go for a moment, Sarah,' he said quickly, and fixed her with the familiar straight blue look. 'I'm glad we met again, because this is the type of question I couldn't ask over the phone. You're not obliged to answer, of course, but there's something I'd like to know.'

Sarah eyed him warily. 'What is it?'

'It's personal,' he warned.

'Go on.'

'Does your little girl's father share your life?'

She shook her head. 'No. He never has.'

His eyes lit with gratifying relief. 'In that case, Sarah Tracy, will you have dinner with me?'

Oh, yes, please, she thought, for the second time in minutes, then gave him an equally straight look. 'If you'll answer a personal question yourself.'

'As many as you like.'

'Just one. Are you married?'

He shook his head, laughing. 'No, Sarah, I'm not. So say yes.'

'Yes, then,' she said, and smiled. 'When did you have in mind?'

'Tonight?'

Sarah stared at him, surprised, and for a moment considered saying she had other plans, just to sound less eager. But only for a split second. 'Yes. Tonight would be fine.'

'Good. I'll call for you at eight.'

Sarah waved as he drove off, then went indoors to find her grandmother coming downstairs, frowning.

'I saw you getting out of a strange car, Sarah. Who brought you home?'

'Jake Hogan.' Sarah looked her grandmother in the eye. 'He asked me out to dinner tonight.'

Margaret's face hardened. 'Are you going? You hardly know the man.'

'I'm going out for a meal, Grandma, not a dirty weekend.'

'Don't be coarse!' Margaret turned to go back upstairs, but Sarah called after her.

'By the way, I had an invitation to Nick Morrell's wedding this morning.'

'Really? If it's when I'm away in Italy I won't be able to look after Davy for you,' was the instant response.

'Actually it's mid-week, when she's in school,' said Sarah, swallowing the angry retort she longed to make. 'I must go. I've got homework to do before I'm free to enjoy myself,' she added deliberately, and gained the hollow victory of knowing her arrow had found its target, by the look on Margaret Parker's face.

But Sarah refused to let the incident affect her buoyant mood as she hurried off to deal with the contents of her briefcase. She could sit in the garden tomorrow. Tonight she was dining out with Jake Hogan.

Work done in record time, Sarah went off to shower in the small bathroom lined with Jake Hogan's Pentiles. After a prolonged session with a hotbrush and all the cosmetic aids at her disposal, she dressed, and, as a gesture of conciliation, went up to her grandmother's sitting room to say she was about to leave. 'Will I do?'

Margaret eyed the linen trousers and amber sleeveless top with surprise. 'You wear that to work.'

'I'm keeping the new dress for Nick's wedding.'

'So you're definitely going, then?'

'Of course I am. You know I'm fond of Nick. I booked a room this morning. Anyway, I haven't a clue where I'm being taken tonight so I thought this rig would do for most places.' She looked her grandmother in the eye. 'And in case you're worried about the expanse of bare flesh I shall wear my jacket all evening even if I fry.'

Although Margaret Parker had been too offended by Sarah's parting shot to wish her a good time, from the moment Sarah opened the door to Jake Hogan she knew the evening would be a success. His fawn linen jacket was creased just enough to look good, and his smile filled her with an anticipation she had never felt before sharing a meal with Brian.

'You look wonderful, Sarah,' Jake informed her.

So did he, but she kept that to herself in case he took it as a come-on. 'Thank you.'

'In this heat I thought you might like a meal in a pub garden tonight,' he said, handing her into his car. 'But if not we could eat at that place near the Pump Rooms in town.'

'I've been there just recently,' she said quickly. For the farewell meal with Brian. 'Eating al fresco sounds wonderful.'

And it was. Jake drove her deep into the Gloucestershire countryside to the Trout Inn, a pretty, unpretentious pub with a stream actually flowing through the garden.

'This is so lovely,' said Sarah, looking round her with pleasure as he led her to the table he'd reserved. 'You knew how I'd choose, then.'

He gave her an outrageously smug smile. 'I booked at the other restaurant, too. I'm a belt and braces kind of guy.'

She laughed. 'What happens when you don't turn up there?'

'I told them to free the table if we hadn't made it by eight-thirty.' He shrugged. 'They were happy. I'm a good customer.'

'You dine there a lot?' she asked, picturing a succession of glamorous companions.

'Lunch mainly, with clients.'

Sarah sat back in her chair while Jake went off to get drinks, putting on mental brakes. She'd only just met the man. Who Jake Hogan entertained to lunch, dinner or breakfast—especially breakfast—was none of her business. Nevertheless, she liked the idea of business clients better than other women. She grinned at her own absurdity, the smile still in her eyes when Jake came back with drinks and a menu.

'You look happy. I'm glad you like it here.'

'It's the kind of place Davy would love, too,' she said, deliberately bringing her child into the conversation.

Jake gave her a questioning look over his glass of beer. 'Did you have to pay someone to stay with her this evening?'

Well done, thought Sarah. Some men changed the subject the moment she mentioned Davy. 'No. She's a weekly boarder at Roedale.'

'Your old school?'

She shook her head. 'At her age I went to the school in the village where I was born. How about you?'

'Liam and I are also products of state education.' He smiled wryly. 'But with differing results. Liam's were uniformly spectacular, mine less so. I joined the family business straight after fairly respectable A-levels. But Liam can boast an Oxford degree, plus an MBA from that high-powered place in France.'

'Impressive,' said Sarah, not sure she liked the sound of Liam Hogan and his credentials.

'Would you mind if I took my jacket off?' Jake asked.

'Not in the least. I'm too warm in mine, too,' she said, ignoring her promise to Margaret.

Jake helped her out of her jacket, eyeing her bare brown shoulders with appreciation. 'You've obviously been on holiday recently.'

She shook her head, smiling. 'Part of it is natural skin tone, the rest fresh air. We've had a heatwave, and I finish work at three. A short session in the garden after work every day is a lot cheaper than a foreign holiday.'

'You obviously never burn.'

'I keep under an umbrella and use sunscreen. After my day in the office I yearn for fresh air.' She leaned back in her chair, relaxed. 'Where do you get *your* tan? Golf?'

'No, genetics. My mother's Italian. We get *our* skin tone from her.'

'Unusual with fair hair.' And very, very appealing to Sarah.

Jake waved a menu at her. 'What do you fancy? Obviously the trout's good.'

'I'll pass on that,' she said hastily. 'My father used to fish for trout when I was young. With far too much success for my liking.'

He laughed. 'Does he still do it?'

'No.' She hesitated. 'Both my parents are dead.'

'I'm sorry.' Jake reached across to touch her hand fleetingly. 'That must be doubly tough on you with a little girl to look after.'

Not a man to shirk sensitive issues, approved Sarah. 'It was at first. Davy was so inconsolable I had to bottle up my own grief to try and help her through it. But don't let's talk of sad things,' she said briskly. 'I don't want to spoil your evening.'

'There's no way you could do that,' he assured her, and tapped the menu. 'So what would you like to start?'

Sarah cast an eye down the list. 'These all sound so tempting. I adore this kind of thing, but if I order one I never get through a main course.'

'Then don't have a main course. I vote we choose two or three starters each, then share the lot.'

'Can we do that?' she said, smiling in delight.

'You can do anything you like,' he assured her softly, with no smile at all.

CHAPTER THREE

PREPARED from the first to enjoy the evening, Sarah found her pleasure increased by the minute as they worked their way through baby asparagus wrapped in parma ham, crab cakes, a *millefeuille* of goat's cheese with roasted red peppers, spicy chorizo sausage, fettucine with smoked salmon, and a platter of home-baked bread. And she was well aware that not all her enjoyment came from the food. The intimate process of dipping into each other's plates was an ice-breaker which rapidly created a rapport between them new to Sarah since her student days.

'Have some bread to fill up the corners,' said Jake, buttering a slice for her.

'This was a brilliant idea,' she assured him indistinctly. 'Are you sure you won't have more corners to fill? This is a pretty light meal by average male standards.'

'I object to the label of average male,' he retorted, grinning. 'Anyway, I ate a large lunch. How about you?'

'I eat a sandwich at my desk every day.' She shrugged. 'As I said, I finish work at three, so I never take a lunch break.'

He frowned as he speared a slice of chorizo. 'Don't you get tired without a proper break?'

'I've been doing it for years. I'm used to it.'

'So, besides work, what else do you do?'

'Cinema, theatre, and so on. Usually with women-

35

friends.' She hesitated. 'And until recently I went out with a man on a more or less regular basis.'

'What happened?'

'He jilted me last Tuesday.'

'Good God, why?' demanded Jake blankly.

Sarah's eyes danced. 'He found someone else. Besides, he felt he wasn't cut out to be a stepfather.'

Jake eyed her searchingly. 'Was there any likelihood of that?'

'Not the remotest chance! It wasn't that kind of relationship. Besides, Davy didn't like him. Though my grandmother did.'

'Is your grandmother's approval vital to you?'

'Fortunately, no, because it's hard to come by where I'm concerned. Her soft spot is reserved for Davy.'

He pushed the asparagus towards her. 'You have that; I'm not keen on it.'

'Really? I love it. I'll swap for the chorizo.' Sarah eyed the plates with respect. 'These are all very generous for starters.' She looked up in sudden suspicion. 'Wait a minute. Did you—?'

'I told them to be generous,' he said, unrepentant. 'At lunch today I was given allegedly king prawns the size of my thumbnail for a first course, so it seemed best to be on the safe side tonight.'

Sarah shook her head, laughing, and applied herself with relish to the asparagus.

'Do you see much of your grandmother?'

'We live with her.' Sarah explained the arrangement in Campden Road.

His lips twitched. 'Did you tell her how we met?'

Sarah laughed. 'I could hardly avoid it. She was there when I arrived looking like a drowned rat.'

His eyes locked on hers. 'I'm sorry I knocked you

over. But on the plus side, if I hadn't I wouldn't have met you. And, as must be perfectly obvious to you, Sarah Tracy, I'm very glad I have.'

'So am I.'

Their eyes held for a couple of heartbeats, then Jake said abruptly, 'How about some pudding? They do a great one here with pecans and honey ice-cream. But you must eat a whole one yourself, or you don't get coffee.'

'I don't want coffee, but I will eat the pudding,' she assured him, because ordering it and waiting for it, and eating it, meant more time spent alone with Jake Hogan in the pretty garden which was empty now, as the evening grew cool. And she had other plans for coffee.

'We could go inside if you're cold,' he offered, as their plates were cleared away.

'I'd much rather stay here.'

'Good. So would I.' He gave the order for their puddings, then moved his chair closer. 'Sarah, maybe it's too soon to ask this, but when you know me better—as I fully intend you shall—you'll find I tend to go straight for what I want.'

Sarah raised an eyebrow. 'That sounds ominous.'

He smiled, his teeth showing white in the dusk. 'Not really. I just want to repeat this kind of evening as soon as possible. Are you by any miracle free this Saturday?'

She shook her head regretfully. 'I'm afraid not.'

Jake leaned closer, his eyes probing. 'You mean you really are tied up, or am I rushing things, taking too much for granted?'

'No,' she said candidly. 'You're not. But this is where problems always arise with my social life. I'm never free at weekends because of Davy.'

'Where was she last Saturday?'

'Enjoying her very first sleepover with a school-friend.'

Jake eyed her thoughtfully. 'But if you live with your grandmother wouldn't she look after Davy for one night?'

'I never leave Davy on the only two nights she spends at home.' Sarah touched her hand to his to emphasise her regret. 'Otherwise, Jake, I'd be only too happy.'

His hand captured hers and held it. 'That's some comfort. But I'm disappointed. Now I shan't know what to do with myself on Saturday.'

'What do you normally do?' she asked, looking at their clasped hands.

'Like you, I also had someone in my life until recently.'

'Just the one?'

'Absolutely. Though there were others in the past before her.' He gave her one of his straight blue looks. 'But just for the record, Sarah, I'm strictly a one woman at a time type.'

She returned the look steadily. 'So what happened with your lady?'

'Like your friend, she preferred someone else—ah, here comes pudding.' Jake released her hand without hurry, but remained close as they ate, chuckling at Sarah's unashamed sounds of appreciation.

'That was wonderful,' she sighed, scraping up the last smear of sauce. 'All of it. In fact I enjoyed this meal more than any I've had in the most expensive hotel in town.'

And not just because of the food.

'So have I.' He leaned closer. 'Did the idiot who jilted you take you to the Chesterton a lot, then?'

'No,' she said, and gave him a demure little smile. 'Brian liked the one near the Pump Rooms.'

'Ah! So that's why you turned it down tonight.'

'Partly. Though when you mentioned eating in a garden it was no contest.'

At last, with a reluctance Sarah shared, Jake got up. 'It's getting cool. Would you like to go inside?'

'Not really. It looks very hot and crowded in there.' She turned to look up at him as he helped her on with her jacket. 'Would you like some coffee at my place instead?'

His smile was answer enough. 'Just give me a minute to settle the bill.'

Sarah's mind worked at top speed while she chatted on the short journey home with Jake. The leap of heat in his eyes at her suggestion warned her to make it clear, without offending him, that coffee meant just coffee. It was not a habit of hers to invite anyone back to share it. Sarah had always met Brian in town, and rarely asked him back to Campden Road to avoid encounters with the all too obviously approving Margaret. Oliver Bryce, the man she'd known before that, had always been in a hurry to get home to the babysitter after their evenings out, so the coffee situation had never arisen with him, either. Not counting visits from college friends, Jake Hogan, if he only knew it, was being granted a rare privilege.

When they arrived Sarah led the way to the sitting room, for the first time that evening ill at ease. 'Do sit down. I shan't be long—'

'Sarah, don't bother with coffee.' Jake caught her by the hand, his eyes very serious. 'Which doesn't mean I'm about to leap on you. I meant I'd sooner have a glass of water.'

She flushed, feeling ridiculous. 'Right. Water it is.'

When she got back with it Jake turned away from the photograph, looked at her closely for a moment, then turned back to study Davy again. 'Exactly the same tortoiseshell eyes and shiny brown hair. Something in the expression, too. The resemblance is remarkable,' he added.

'Would you like to take off your jacket?' she asked, to attract his attention away from Davina.

Jake put his glass on the table near the lilies he'd sent her, and removed his jacket, his eyes teasing as he grinned at Sarah. 'Relax,' he ordered. 'I never ravish a lady on a first date, I swear.'

Sarah laughed awkwardly, feeling her colour rise. 'I'm glad to hear it. Won't you sit down?'

'Yes,' he said promptly. 'If you will, too.' He took her hand and drew her down beside him on her sofa. 'Now, tell me why you're on edge, Sarah. Bad experiences in this situation before?'

'No, not at all.' She braced herself. 'I've never asked anyone back here before.'

He gave her an incredulous look. 'Never? How long have you lived here?'

'Nearly four years.'

'Is this because your grandmother shares the house?'

'Not really. She converted the house into separate flats for the express purpose of privacy for both of us.'

Jake took her hand. 'I'm hoping against hope I know the answer, Sarah, but why me?'

Sarah shrugged. 'I was enjoying the evening, and it's not very late, so it just seemed the natural thing to do.'

His grasp tightened. 'Actually, you pre-empted me. I was just about to suggest coffee at my place. Would you have come?'

She smiled a little. 'You didn't ask so we'll never know.'

'I'll ask next time,' he warned.

'Is there going to be a next time?'

'Damn right there is,' he said, and kissed her. Then stared in astonishment as she immediately scrambled out of reach, her face flaming at the blank surprise on his face as he promptly removed himself to the other end of the sofa.

'I meant what I said,' Jake assured her. 'No ravishing on the first date, Sarah. Just a kiss, I swear.' He drew in a deep, unsteady breath. 'Though from my point of view it was a rash move to share our meal in that particular way.'

Afraid to trust her voice for a moment, Sarah raised a questioning eyebrow, and Jake smiled wryly.

'I meant, Miss Tracy, that for me the entire meal was a subtle form of foreplay. Couldn't you tell?'

'No. I thought we were just getting on well together.' She hesitated. 'So if you had asked me back to your place, and I'd agreed, you would have taken it for granted I was saying yes to a whole lot more than coffee?'

'No, Sarah, absolutely not.' Jake stood up, holding out a hand to help her to her feet. 'Like you, I simply wanted to prolong our time together.'

She looked up into his eyes. And believed him.

'So when can I see you again?' he went on, as though the awkward little incident had never happened. 'You said Saturday's out, but how about Sunday evening?'

Sarah felt an overwhelming rush of relief. She had been so sure Jake would give up on her after her embarrassing little rejection. She couldn't tell him that if she'd followed her instincts she would have let him kiss her as much as he wanted. Because with him she wanted it too. But that way danger lay. As she knew better than most, instincts had to be reined in, not followed blindly. Yet even on such short acquaintance she was sure that Jake would never force her to anything. And she wanted to see him again. She always felt a bit down after taking Davy back to school. Time spent with Jake Hogan would be the perfect antidote to her usual Sunday evening blues.

'Yes. I'd like that,' she said at last.

'That took a long time,' he said dryly. 'What shall we do?'

She smiled at him. 'If it's fine I'd like a drive to somewhere pleasant with a view, then a long, leisurely walk.'

'That's a first,' said Jake, laughing. 'No lady in my past ever asked to go hiking before.'

'No hiking—just a Sunday evening stroll, please!'

'Whatever you want. What time do you get back from Davy's school?'

'About six.'

'I'll be here soon after, then.' He looked down at her for a moment, then bent and kissed her forehead. 'Goodnight, Sarah Tracy.'

'Goodnight, Jake Hogan.' She stepped back, her eyes suddenly serious. 'Thank you for this evening. I enjoyed it very much.'

'So did I.' Jake followed her to the front door. 'Next time you can introduce me to your grandmother,' he said with a grin, and crossed the pavement to his car.

Sarah watched him get in, raised her hand in response to his wave as he drove off, then went back in the house and closed the door, her eyes wistful. The man was a charmer. Unlike comfortable, friendly Oliver, or staid, unimpassioned Brian, it would be all too easy to fall in love with Jake Hogan.

CHAPTER FOUR

SARAH was about to leave the office on Friday afternoon to collect Davy, when Alison Rogers rang her cellphone number.

'Sarah, I'm in a fix. My car won't start, and Don's in London until tonight—'

'No problem, I'll pick Polly up,' said Sarah promptly. 'You just caught me; I'm on my way right now.'

'You're an angel! I'll ring the school and let them know. See you soon—I'll have tea and buns waiting.'

When Sarah collected them later Polly and Davina were in tearing spirits to be going home together, and full of their practice for sports day. They piled into the car, straw boaters askew, gingham dresses rumpled, both of them excited because Davy had beaten everyone in her class in the sprint.

'But Polly came second at skipping,' added Davy.

'Well done, both of you!'

Polly smiled at Sarah expectantly. 'Are you staying to tea? Mummy always bakes stuff on Friday, ready for when I come home.'

'Please can we?' urged Davy, hovering as Sarah stowed their belongings away.

'Yes, but we won't stay long. I'm sure Polly's mummy saw quite enough of you last weekend. Now, tell me what else you two have been up to this week, besides races. How about boring stuff like sums, and so on?'

When they arrived at the Rogers house, Alison came

running out to greet them. 'You saved my life,' she said gratefully, after embracing her daughter. 'Take Davy off to wash hands, Polly. Sit down, Sarah,' she added, 'you look tired. Hard day?'

'No more than usual. It's just a rush on Fridays to get off on time to drive to Roedale.'

'Davy told me you work at home in the evenings as well.'

'Part of the deal with my employers. It only takes up an hour or so.' Sarah shrugged, smiling. 'In my circumstances the arrangement's very convenient. When Davy's home I work after she's gone to bed.'

'Hard graft just the same.' Alison put plates of cupcakes and cookies on the table, went to call the girls, then sat down to pour tea.

'Thank you,' said Sarah, accepting her cup. 'I rang my grandmother before I left to tell her we'd be later today.'

'I've heard a lot about Grandma. Though I thought she was your mother.'

'No, she dotes on Davy, but she's actually *my* grandmother.'

Davina came running in with Polly, very much at home in her friend's house. The girls polished off several cakes and cookies, swallowed down large glasses of the milk Davy always objected to at home, then rushed out to play in the garden.

'Peace at last,' said Alison with satisfaction, and refilled Sarah's cup. 'Have another cookie to assuage my guilt.'

'Why guilt?' said Sarah, amused.

'It suddenly struck me that you'll be picking Polly up *next* week as well.'

'I don't mind in the least. But I'll have that cookie. They're delicious.'

'With the life you lead I don't suppose you get much time for baking,' said Alison with sympathy.

Sarah shook her head, laughing. 'Actually, I do. Since Davy started boarding I have a lot more time to myself, socially and otherwise. But no baking. I'm hopeless at it. Lucky for us, my grandmother's an expert. She also makes Sunday lunch for the three of us.' Sarah smiled. 'But during the week I fend for myself, or go out. Something I do a lot more than I used to now Davy's in school. Beforehand I hated the thought of parting with her, even on a weekly basis, but now she's settled in I confess I'm rather enjoying my new freedom.'

When she was finally able to tear Davy away Sarah drove home to find a message on her machine, but she sent Davy off to find Margaret before she allowed herself to listen to it.

'Jake, Sarah,' said familiar tones. 'Just reminding you about Sunday.'

As if she needed reminding! But she played the message again twice, just to listen to his voice. Like a schoolgirl with a first crush, she thought sheepishly.

Margaret came down with Davy to announce that she was going out shortly, and had taken the liberty of making the sauce for their pasta supper.

Davy's eyes lit up. 'With lots of tomato in it? Goody.'

'Thank you, Grandma,' said Sarah shortly. 'But I could have managed.'

'Out of a jar, no doubt,' said Margaret, after Davy rushed off to change. 'By the way,' she added coldly, 'more flowers came for you today. I put them in water in the kitchen.'

'Who are they from?' said Sarah, surprised.

'I've no idea. The card was addressed to you.'

Sarah hurried to the kitchen to take a card from the envelope propped beside an enormous bunch of brilliantly coloured zinnias. 'They're from Jake Hogan,' she told her grandmother, who had followed behind to find out.

'Again,' commented Margaret. 'He obviously enjoyed the evening with you.'

'We both did. I asked him in when he drove me home.'

'You've never done that before,' said Margaret accusingly.

'Don't worry. He didn't stay long.'

'I know. I heard him leave.'

'Then you know exactly how long he stayed,' said Sarah evenly.

Margaret's mouth tightened. 'I don't mean to be hard on you, Sarah, but you're obviously attracted to this man, so do please be careful. Try to look at things from my point of view.'

'Oh, I do. All the time.' Their eyes clashed for a moment. 'But sometimes, Grandma, try to remember that I have a point of view too.'

Davy talked non-stop through supper in the kitchen with Sarah, giving her a blow by blow account of every minute at school during the week. 'It's nice to be home, though,' she said, with a heartfelt sigh.

Sarah gave her a searching look. 'I thought you were liking school better these days.'

Davy nodded vigorously. 'I am. But I still like being home with you best.'

Sarah gave her a hug. 'You do your stuff in front of

the TV while I clear up, then we'll watch a video. *Father Goose*, if you like.'

The film was one of Davy's favourites. And, because there was no such thing as too much Cary Grant for Sarah, they both enjoyed their evening together, as usual. But Davy sighed mutinously when Sarah rewound the video tape.

'I suppose you've got work to do now.'

'Afraid so. But it's time you were asleep anyway. It's way past school bedtime.'

'Which is why I prefer it at home!'

Next day Davy was up early, eager to make the most of every minute as usual, and after breakfast Sarah took her into town for the usual programme of a swim at the leisure centre pool, followed by shopping for new jeans before Davy's invariable choice of a pizza lunch.

'What would you like to do now?' asked Sarah, as they left the restaurant. 'It seems a shame to sit in a cinema on an afternoon like this. There's a craft fair on in the park.'

'Hot dogs and doughnuts?' said Davy hopefully.

'Probably. Though how you can even think about them straight after lunch beats me,' said Sarah, laughing.

'I've had a week of school dinners! Let's go.'

As they strolled together through the town centre Sarah caught sight of their reflections in a shop window, and with regret realised that her child was growing up very fast. Davy, as usual, chattered nineteen to the dozen as they walked, her face animated in the frame of bright brown hair still damp round the edges from her swim.

'Next year there's a school trip to France,' Davy said eventually, and gave Sarah a hopeful glance. 'Will I be able to go?'

'Of course,' said Sarah without hesitation, though extras of this kind meant a lot of creative juggling with her finances. 'But thank you for giving me due warning.'

'I don't have to go,' said Davy bravely.

'Of course you do. I can have some peace and quiet without you.'

Davy giggled, then tugged Sarah's arm. 'There's a man waving at you over there, Mummy.'

Sarah's heart gave a thump when she saw Jake crossing the road towards them.

'Who's that?' whispered Davy.

'A friend,' Sarah whispered before he reached them. 'Be nice.'

'Hello, Sarah.' Jake smiled at her, then turned his attention to Davy. 'Hi, there. I'm Jake Hogan.'

Sarah, prepared to give a surreptitious dig to prompt a polite response, was surprised to see Davy return Jake's smile far more pleasantly than she'd ever managed with Brian.

'Hello, I'm Davy Tracy,' she told him. 'Well, Davina, really. But Mummy only says that when she's cross.'

'I know all about that,' he assured her. 'When my mother calls me Jacob I shake in my shoes.'

Davy's eyes widened. 'Even though you're grown up?'

'Especially now I'm grown up!' He turned to Sarah. 'Are you out for a walk, or can I give you both a lift somewhere?'

'That's very kind of you,' she said, smiling, 'but we're not going home yet. We went for a swim, had lunch, and now we're making for the show in the park.'

Sarah was tempted to ask him to join them. But from past experience with Brian she knew that Davy would probably object to having a stranger muscle in on her precious Saturday.

'Sounds like fun,' said Jake. 'Enjoy yourselves. Nice to meet you, Davy.' He smiled at Sarah, hesitated a moment, then with one of his straight blue looks said goodbye and went off in the opposite direction before she could thank him for the flowers.

'Is that a new friend?' asked Davy, as they made for the park.

'Yes. I met him quite recently. Why?'

'He's cool. Not a bit like Boring Brian,' said Davy, then made a face. 'Sorry!'

'I should think so,' said Sarah, trying not to laugh. 'And for your information, miss, I don't go out with Brian any more.'

'Really?' Davy's face lit up. 'Is that because of Mr Hogan?'

'Certainly not. Brian and I decided to call it a day, that's all.'

Davy danced a little jig of jubilation. 'Great! I was really, really afraid you were going to marry Brian and I'd have to call him Daddy.'

Sarah couldn't help laughing. 'There was never any question of that, muggins.'

'Thank goodness. Not that I'd mind if you did get married one day,' added Davy magnanimously. 'Someone like Polly's dad would be fab.'

'I'll keep it in mind!'

Davy loved everything about the afternoon, delighted when she found that a dog show was part of the entertainment. She went into raptures over the irresistible Labradors, and clapped the elegant, obedient German Shepherds, then went wild with excitement when teams of mongrels raced against each other through obstacle courses. In between events she downed a hot dog, and several doughnuts, and after a few determined attempts knocked down enough skittles to win a small white rab-bit with blue eyes.

'Do you think Grandma would like this?' she asked, as they eventually began trudging home.

'That's a nice thought. I'm sure she'll love it.'

'That's for me?' said Margaret with delight when Davy handed it over. 'And you won it? Thank you so much, darling. What's his name?'

Davy gave Sarah a wide, wicked grin. 'How about Jake?'

Sarah gave her a kindling look and despatched her off for a bath. 'You reek of doughnuts, young lady.'

'So does this rabbit,' observed Margaret, when Davy was out of earshot. 'Why Jake?'

Sarah explained their chance encounter with Jake Hogan. 'She told me she likes him more than Boring Brian.'

Margaret gave a reluctant laugh. 'Oh, dear. "Out of the mouth of babes", and all that.'

Sarah gave her a narrowed look. 'Are you telling me you agree with her? Yet you wanted me to marry Brian.'

Her grandmother passed a hand over her immaculate hair, looking defensive. 'I just want security for you, Sarah.'

'*If* I ever marry, which is unlikely in my particular circumstances, I'm fool enough to want a whole lot more than mere security.' Sarah yawned suddenly. 'Sorry. I need to scrub the reek of fast food from my person.'

When Davy was safely delivered back to Roedale next day the entire process was a lot happier than usual for Sarah, with the prospect of Jake's company to look for-ward to. Right from Davy's first day at Roedale Sarah had made a habit of taking herself to bed early on Sundays to get the evening over with.

But tonight, she thought jubilantly, I'll be with Jake— and slammed on the mental brakes again when the thought triggered off alarm bells. Careful, she warned herself.

But when Sarah turned into Campden Road she saw Jake leaning against the bonnet of his car, waiting for her, and knew that the alarm bells had rung too late. It would be all too easy to fall madly in love with Jake Hogan. She was halfway there already, if she were honest with herself. And because this particular form of madness had never troubled her before the early-warning signs had gone unnoticed.

Almost before she'd stopped the car Jake opened her door to help her out. 'At last. I made the mistake of turning up early. I was getting impatient.'

'Hi,' she said, smiling. 'Come in for a minute.'

Jake followed her through the front door, closed it behind him, then glanced at the stairs. 'Is your grand- mother in?'

'No. Why?'

He took her in his arms very carefully and, when she didn't resist, let out a deep breath and held her close. 'Because I've been wanting this since I left you on Friday night,' he whispered. 'But don't worry, I won't kiss you unless you ask me nicely. Even though I wanted to kiss you when we met yesterday, too. Could you tell?'

She flushed. 'No, of course not.'

'Were you pleased to see me?'

'Yes. So pleased I forgot to thank you for the flowers,' she said breathlessly.

He grinned down at her. 'Or were you too chicken to mention them because Davy was with you?'

'Not at all.' She smiled. 'But you don't have to keep sending me flowers, Jake.'

'Why not?' he said casually, and released her, his eyes alight with something which made Sarah back away.

'If we're going walking we'd better get moving,' she said hurriedly. 'So read the Sunday papers for a minute, Jake, while I park the car.'

'Where?'

'There's a garage at the bottom of the garden.'

'Give me your keys and I'll do it.'

Sarah gave instructions about the lane running behind Campden Road, told Jake to come back through the garden, and while he was gone rushed to add a few touches to the face which glowed at her from the mirror. She changed her school-visit linen skirt and leather slingbacks for pink cotton jeans and powder-blue suede loafers, then hurried to the back door just as Jake appeared outside.

'Thank you,' she said, taking her keys. 'The car stays there now until I fetch Davy next Friday.'

'So what happens if you get caught in a thunderstorm on the way home from work again?' he demanded.

'I shall study weather forecasts with more attention in future.'

'Do you have a cellphone?'

'Yes.'

'Good. If you're in any doubt ring me and I'll drive you home.'

Sarah's eyes danced. 'What happens if your secretary tells me Mr Hogan's too busy to talk to me?'

'I'll give strict instructions to the contrary. And before I bring you back tonight we'll exchange numbers.' He gave her the familiar look. 'Ring mine any time you want, night or day, Sarah. Now, let's go for that walk.'

Jake drove her to the outskirts of town to park outside a restaurant which had once been a railway station. 'We'll leave the car here while we stroll along the walkway they've made along the track. It used to be a local branch line once. They do rather good home-made food during the day. Have you never been here before?'

Sarah shook her head. 'Not since the makeover. But I will in future. Davy could even ride her bike along here.'

'I bring the kids here sometimes, with theirs,' he told her, and laughed at the look on her face. 'I own to a couple of sisters, too, both of them married with a brace of children each.'

'Ah! So that's why you were so relaxed with Davy.'

'It wasn't hard. She's a cute little girl.'

'Don't say little in front of her, please! Davy thinks she's pretty grown up.' Sarah pulled a face. 'We had quite an argument over clothes yesterday. She tried to con me into buying her some utterly gruesome shoes, as worn by her favourite pop star.'

'Did you give in?'

'No. I compromised. An art I'm learning with Davy now she's growing up so fast. I let her have the embroidered jeans she wanted, but not the shoes. She must respect the line I draw.' Sarah smiled up at him. 'Which she does, most of the time.'

'Maddy's girls go running to their father if she says no—' Jake halted, his eyes dark with remorse. 'Hell, Sarah—I'm *sorry*.'

'Don't be. I'm not the least sensitive on the subject,' she assured him, with a smile designed to convince him she meant it. 'So, tell me how your sister's husband copes with feminine wiles.'

'Sam learned early on to turn a deaf ear to his daughters in preference to getting a black eye from his wife. My sister inherited my mother's temper. Paula's boys are older, and more interested in electronic gear than clothes.'

'It must be fun, being part of a big family,' she said enviously.

Jake shrugged. 'Fun sometimes, mayhem at others. Those of us who live locally are expected to turn up regularly for Sunday lunch with my parents. Liam, too, now and then. My mother doesn't regard living in London as an impediment to visiting the family.'

'Is your brother married?'

'No. But attached. Temporarily.'

Sarah raised an eyebrow at his tone. 'You don't like the lady?'

'Liam does, which is more to the point.' Jake glanced at his watch. 'Come on, let's go back to my place and have some supper.'

'I had a big lunch,' she warned him. 'My grandmother cooks for us on Sunday, and demands clean plates.'

'I'm sure you can find room for some of my mother's cannelloni. She sends me home with something from her freezer every time I visit, convinced I don't eat properly.'

'And do you?'

'I did the other night,' he said quietly. He cast a glance along the leafy, deserted walkway, then took her hands and brought her round to face him. 'I keep thinking of the way we shared the meal, Sarah Tracy.'

She looked up at him steadily. 'So do I.'

He looked at her mouth, shook his head with regret, and began to walk with her again. 'This was a very good idea of yours. I spend far too much time cooped up in places with recycled air. Next time,' he went on, 'we could bring Davy.'

Sarah shook her head firmly. 'I'd rather not involve Davy in my social life.'

Jake frowned. 'Why? Because your recent friend jilted you?'

'Not at all. Davy was delighted about that.' Sarah gave a sudden chuckle. 'Apparently she'd been horribly afraid I'd marry Boring Brian and she'd have to call him Daddy.'

Jake gave a shout of laughter that attracted amused glances from a couple passing by with a dog. 'And is he boring?'

'I suppose so, a little. Which is why I was about to let him down gently and call it a day. But before I could he took the wind out of my sails by dumping me instead.' Sarah laughed ruefully. 'Which cut me down to size pretty effectively!'

'The man's an idiot,' said Jake dismissively, then shot her a glance. 'Is Davy opposed to marriage altogether, then, where you're concerned?'

'Not at all. She informed me on Saturday that she fancies a daddy like Polly's, for preference.'

'How does Polly's daddy feel about that?'

Sarah chuckled. 'It's her mummy who would raise objections, I imagine, so because I like Alison Rogers very much I'll pass on that one.'

Jake halted. 'You don't mean Don Rogers's wife?'

'Yes. Do you know her?'

'I certainly do. Her husband's firm deals with my legal affairs. Good man, Don.'

'Small world!'

'In this town it's unavoidable. In fact,' added Jake as

they resumed their stroll, 'it's strange I haven't run into you before.'

Sarah laughed. 'Unfortunate turn of phrase! But it's not surprising we haven't met. I didn't go out much socially until last autumn.'

'What happened then?'

'Davy started at Roedale. Before that all the time left over from my job was spent in chauffeuring her to various after-school things, like ballet and swimming lessons, overseeing homework, and just being there for her.'

When they got to the car Jake handed her in, looking thoughtful. 'And was that enough for you, Sarah?'

'I've had a pretty normal social life during the last few months,' she told him as he slid in beside her. 'There was someone else before Brian.'

'If you tell me that guy broke up with you as well I just won't believe it.'

'No. I managed to get in first with Oliver.'

'It wasn't working with him, either?'

'No.'

'Why not?'

'He was a widower, for a start—'

'And Davy didn't like him?'

'She never met him.' Sarah shrugged. 'Oliver has a small son. And because I refused to involve Davy in outings as a foursome it died a natural death. Besides, the poor man still hankered after his dead wife.'

Jake drove in silence for a moment, then gave her a swift, sidelong look. 'Just for the record, Sarah, I don't hanker after anyone.'

She was very glad to hear it. 'Not even the lady you mentioned?'

'No. I own to siblings and parents who sometimes

interfere in my life, but generally speaking I'm not bringing much excess baggage to our relationship, Sarah.'

Relationship?

'I've obviously stricken you dumb,' he said after a while. 'Is the idea so unattractive to you, then? The moment I saw you—'

'I was soaking wet and screaming at you in fury,' she reminded him.

He shrugged. 'I knew, just the same.'

'Knew what?'

'That I wanted you in my life. So I sent flowers and came hammering on your door. And when you finally opened it, I stood transfixed.'

'Because I looked so much better dry?'

'You clean up well,' he agreed with a grin, then turned a wry blue look in her direction. 'But then I saw Davy's photograph and assumed you were married. Surely you noted my relief when you said you were *Miss* Tracy?'

She gave him a thoughtful glance. 'How old are you, Jake?'

'Thirty. Why?'

'You're successful, and no turn-off in the looks department. So why aren't *you* married? Or at least spoken for.'

'I've never even come near to it. No sinister reason, I swear,' he added. 'I'm straight, by the way, in case you had doubts.'

'None at all,' she assured him, smiling.

Jake parked the car outside his apartment block and took her hands, his eyes very serious as they held hers. 'Right. So when it comes to a relationship I meant you could choose any kind you want, Sarah, as long as it includes me.'

CHAPTER FIVE

JAKE'S home was a large modern apartment with a balcony overlooking the River Penn. Big windows and gleaming wood floors, walls painted uniformly cream and almost bare of ornament, were all a far cry from the gloomy, crowded old house Sarah shared with her grandmother.

'Have you been here long?' asked Sarah, entranced by the light and space.

'You mean it looks bare?'

She shook her head. 'I like it a lot.'

He looked pleased. 'When I first got a place of my own I lived in a furnished flat in a house very much like yours. A move which mystified my mother, who couldn't see why I had to leave the comforts of home. Eventually I heard along the grapevine that this was coming on the market, and I was lucky enough to snap it up straight away. But I'm proceeding gradually with furniture, buying things when I find them. And at the same time trying not to offend my mother, who desperately wants to help.'

'Why not let her?'

Jake smiled ruefully. 'Her taste runs to pictures and mirrors and cushions, and every inch of floor space covered by carpet. Which is fine in my parents' house. But definitely not here.'

Sarah nodded, deeply envious as she looked at the fringed Art Nouveau rug in subtle shades of chestnut and rose, chairs and sofa upholstered in suede the colour of honey to echo the leather metal-studded screen in a corner. Niches had been fitted with downlighters and glass shelves, but the latter were empty except for a solitary bronze nude.

'Liam gave me that as a moving-in present,' Jake told her. He leaned against a wall, arms folded, watching Sarah's face as she took time to look at everything before moving across the room to admire the view.

'No curtains,' she commented, noting the blind furled away at windows that slid open on to a balcony.

'That came with the flat. It looked good to me, so I left it.'

'You were right.' She turned to smile at him. 'It's a shame to hide the view.'

'There's a good one in here, too, only smaller,' he informed her, showing her into a kitchen fitted out with beechwood and stainless steel, and a window with a different angle on the river.

'This room doesn't look used much!' she commented.

Jake smiled. 'I did some hectic tidying up this morning to impress you.'

Sarah *was* impressed. By everything in Jake's home. 'Don't you have someone in to clean?'

'Never on Sundays.' He gave her the straight look which usually presaged some equally straight talking. 'You don't have to inspect the bedroom, by the way. It's not an obligatory part of the tour.'

'Of course I do,' she said briskly. 'I've heard a lot about this place, but I've never been in one of the apartments. I want to see everything—especially the bathroom. I assume it's done out in the very best Pentiles can provide?'

Jake took her to inspect it. 'I had it altered before I moved in. The former tenant put in a sort of Roman sunken bath with a mosaic backdrop up to the ceiling. To me it looked like the communal bath we all jumped in after rugby matches at school. I couldn't live with it.' He smiled. 'I was pleased the man used Pentiles for the purpose when he had it done originally, of course, but I swapped it all for conventional fittings, and a minimum of Pentiles' finest round the bath.'

'No power shower?' said Sarah in mock disapproval.

'That's in my own bathroom. Come through the bedroom and take a look.'

Sarah was unsurprised to find walls and even the linen on the wide bed all in the same uniform cream. A fitted carpet in tawny wool added a note of warmth, but, not counting the built-in cupboards which housed Jake's clothes, the only piece of furniture was a solitary bedside table with a bronze lamp. The effect should have been spartan in such a large room. But when she thought of her own room at Campden Road, with her desk and computer crammed in with the bedroom furniture brought from her family home, she envied Jake the space and tranquillity. Envied him the entire flat, she thought with a sigh, as he opened a door on the far side of the room so she could take a quick look at the shower housed in bronze glass.

'So. What's the verdict?' he asked as they went back to the kitchen.

'I'm green with envy,' she said frankly.

Jake looked pleased as he hooked a leather-topped kitchen stool over to the window. 'Gaze at sunset on the river for a while—I shan't be long.'

'Can't I help?'

'No. Just sit there looking decorative while I work.' Jake took the cork from a bottle of wine. 'Shall I throw a salad together?'

Sarah shook her head, smiling. 'Not for me. I eat so much of it lately I'll pass on that for once, Jake, thanks. But some bread would be good.'

'My mother gave me a loaf baked with her own fair hand. So in a minute we'll take all this into the other room and picnic. Because, as you may have noticed, I don't possess a dining room.'

'Would you use one much if you did?' she asked.

'Probably not. There was a dining room originally, but the Roman bath tenant did away with it to make one big living space. Right,' he added, as the timer went off, 'if you'll take the wine and the glasses, I'll bring the tray. Then I'll come back for our cannelloni.'

When Jake handed her a steaming, savoury plateful Sarah received it doubtfully. 'Shouldn't we eat this out on the balcony? I'd hate to mark this upholstery.'

'It won't matter if you do. The suede is man-made and guaranteed, I was assured, to repel stains. So far it's keeping its word.'

They sat together on the sofa, which Jake pulled nearer the window to watch the sunset. And though the cannelloni was delicious, and Sarah possessed more appetite for it than she'd expected, she knew perfectly well that, just like the evening at the Trout Inn, it was Jake's company that made the meal special.

'That was wonderful,' she said at last, as she mopped up sauce with her bread. 'Your mother's a great cook.'

'I thought of trying to impress you by pretending I'd made the cannelloni myself,' Jake confessed, grinning. 'But I stuck with the truth.' He refilled her glass, then got up to take their plates. When he came back he settled beside her with a sigh of content. 'So what do you usually do after you've taken Davy back on Sunday evenings?'

'Mope a lot and go to bed early with a book.' Sarah smiled at him. 'This is a *great* improvement.'

'Thank you.' Jake moved nearer and slid an arm round her shoulders. 'It's a big improvement on my Sunday evenings, too.'

'What do you normally do?' she asked, resisting an urge to lay her head on his shoulder.

'Nothing much. After family lunch I talk shop with my father, then I come back here and get stuck into some paperwork.'

Sarah turned her head to look up at him. 'Every Sunday?'

The thick lashes descended like shutters. 'Lately, yes. Before that I spent my weekends in London for a while. Not that many, as it turned out.'

'Why not?'

'As I told you, she met someone else,' he said shortly.

Something in his tone made Sarah uneasy. 'I really must be going,' she said, getting to her feet. 'Thank you for supper.'

He leapt up, frowning in surprise. 'Don't go yet. I didn't mean to snap.' He put a hand on hers. 'Look. I said I wasn't bringing any baggage to our relationship, Sarah, and I meant it.'

She gave him a look as straight as his. 'We don't have a relationship—'

'Of course we do. Admit it.'

'All right. But we won't if you still hanker after the lady.'

'There's no question of that.' Jake touched a hand to her cheek. 'Come and sit down again so I can explain. Then, if you still want me to, I'll drive you home.'

Jake switched on a couple of lamps and resumed his place beside her. But this time he kept his distance.

'I met the lady in question in London,' he began, staring out into the darkening sky.

Sarah gave him a hostile look. Couldn't he even bring himself to mention her name?

'We were both after the same taxi, so we shared it, and things went on from there pretty rapidly,' Jake continued. 'She works in advertising, earns a lot of money, and loathes the country. I could never persuade her to come down here. So I went up to her place at weekends instead. Then before you could even call the arrangement a habit she met someone else. End of story.'

'But you still care?' asked Sarah quietly.

Jake's head swivelled, his eyes bright with surprise. 'Good God, no. I was bloody angry at the time, but if you mean was my heart broken, definitely not. It was never that kind of thing.'

'Then what kind of thing was it?'

His eyes remained steady. 'A fling, pure and simple.'

'So why do you mind so much?'

'Because she lied to me. Kept me on a string even though she fancied someone else. It was the other man who insisted she tell me.'

'So why hadn't she told you before?'

'She said,' replied Jake sardonically, 'that she couldn't bring herself to hurt me, which was a bit dramatic when all we'd had together were a couple of weekends of wining and dining. And bed, of course. Not earth-shattering stuff, by any stretch of the imagination. Any of it. When I pointed this out she lost it and slapped my face, at which point I lost *my* temper, stormed out of her flat and drove home.' He was silent for a moment, his eyes absent, then smiled at Sarah in apology. 'Sorry! I didn't mean to bore you with my past.' He slid closer and kissed her before she could dodge away. 'I had a very different plan in mind for you for this evening,' he whispered.

She sprang up, eyeing him in suspicion. 'Plan?'

'Turn of phrase, nothing more,' he said, taken aback. 'I just wanted to spend time getting to know you better.'

With a session in bed at the end of it? Sarah's chin lifted. 'I think I will go home now, please.'

Jake rose to his feet, frowning. 'Why so soon? If I swear not to lay a finger on you, Sarah, will you stay for a while?'

She shook her head, refusing to meet his eyes. 'It's getting late; we both have work tomorrow—'

'And suddenly you just can't wait to get away.' He looked at her in silence for a moment, giving her time to change her mind. When it was obvious this wasn't going to happen he shrugged negligently, his eyes suddenly cold. 'Let's go, then.'

Sarah sat silent on the way home, cursing her ingrained tendency to take flight at the first hint of sexual danger. This time it had spoiled an evening which up to then had been idyllic. The walk, the meal had been perfect. Then the mere mention of bed had ruined everything.

When they arrived in Campden Road Jake pointedly left the engine running. He got out of the car, and with punctilious courtesy helped her out, then saw her to her door, brushed aside her thanks for the meal, and drove off.

Sarah spent a very restless night afterwards. Had she really expected Jake to beg her to stay? Fond hope! The easy charm was a very effective disguise for the steel underneath. Not that it mattered any more, because she'd blown any chance of getting to know him better. All because Jake Hogan had uttered the buzz words 'plan' and 'bed'. And to cap it all they hadn't exchanged tele-phone numbers after all.

No more a lover of Mondays than anyone else, Sarah found her prevailing mood of deep depression made the next day so much harder to bear than usual that her colleagues even asked if she were coming down with something. To demonstrate that she wasn't she drove herself so hard that in addition to her usual work she finished most of the day's correspondence during office hours, then stayed on late to finish the rest.

When Sarah emerged into rain pouring down from a sky as dark as her mood, she trudged along under an umbrella, wondering why on earth she'd polished off the mail in the office when there was a whole evening yawn-ing ahead of her with nothing to do. She was sunk so deep in gloom she jumped yards at a touch on her arm, and whirled round to come face to face with Jake Hogan. He looked tall and unfamiliar in a belted raincoat, a drip-ping hat pulled down over eyes that held none of their usual smiling warmth.

'You worked late today,' he said, without greeting.

'Hello, Jake,' Sarah retorted pointedly, to disguise how utterly delighted she was to see him. 'What are you doing here?'

'Waiting for you, and getting drenched for my pains. I'll drive you home.' Without waiting for consent he took her arm to hurry her to the car waiting at the kerb, but said nothing about his reason for waiting for her. They were halfway to Campden Road before Sarah could bring herself to break the silence between them.

'I'm sorry about last night,' she said at last, staring at the rain sluicing down the windscreen.

'So am I.' He slanted a baffled look at her. 'What the hell did I *do*?'

'You said you like the truth,' she said after a while.

'Normally, yes,' agreed Jake heavily. 'This time, probably not.'

Spit it out, Sarah told herself. Get it over with. 'You said you wanted to be part of my life in whatever way I chose.'

He nodded, his face sombre. 'I did. And I meant it.' He parked the car outside the house, took off the hat, tossed it into the back seat, then turned to look at her. 'I still mean it.'

Sarah returned the look steadily. 'Jake, how long did your association with the advertising lady last?'

His eyes narrowed. 'Not very long at all. Three—no, four—weekends. Probably no more than ten days or so, all told.'

'But right from the start you were sleeping together?'

Jake's eyes lit with sudden comprehension. 'Yes. I went to stay in her flat, and she took it for granted I'd share her bed.' He shrugged. 'It's common enough practice, Sarah.'

'So common that bed was the plan you had for me last night, too?'

Jake stared at her in brooding silence for so long Sarah was on the point of getting out of the car when he finally spoke.

'You mean you can't bear the thought of that, Sarah? With me?'

'No,' she admitted, flushing. 'I don't mean that at all. But it's not going to happen just the same, Jake. No bed. Just friendship.'

He took her hand. 'You might change your mind as you get to know me better.'

'I wouldn't count on it.' Sarah looked away. 'I enjoy your company, but that's as far as it goes, Jake.'

He put a finger under her chin and brought her round to look at him, the hard planes of his face softened a little. 'Is it a case of once bitten, twice shy, Sarah?'

She nodded mutely, taking refuge in an explanation he could accept.

Jake took her hand in a firm, warm clasp. 'I still want to spend time with you, Sarah.'

'I want that, too,' she assured him.

He relaxed visibly. 'So what are you doing tonight?'

'Nothing much.'

The brooding look disappeared, replaced by the sudden familiar smile which breached every defence she possessed. 'There's a Clint Eastwood film on at the Regal. If I promise—Scouts' honour—just to hold your hand, will you come?'

Sarah's smile matched Jake's, her dark mood suddenly vanished. 'An offer I can't resist. Will you throw in popcorn?'

'Ice-cream, too, if you're good.'

'Done!'

They went to the cinema together that night, and held hands, just as Jake had promised. And when he drove Sarah home he gave her a brief goodnight kiss in the car, then saw her to her door. He took her to dinner at the Chesterton the following evening, and to the theatre later in the week to see the local repertory company tackling Ibsen. But when Jake brought her home after the play the brooding look reappeared when they arrived in Campden Road.

'I suppose that's it until next week, then?'

'Afraid so.' Sarah chuckled. 'If I live that long! Tomorrow Davy's bringing Polly home with her for the weekend. After which we take Polly back and join the

Rogers family for Sunday lunch.' She smiled at him. 'I'm really looking forward to that.'

'Will you be up to seeing me on Sunday evening afterwards?'

'Probably not,' she said with regret. 'I may just want to crawl into bed.'

Jake frowned. 'Which means Wednesday before I see you again. I'm away on Monday, and I'll be tied up until late on Tuesday evening.'

Sarah eyed him in dismay. 'And Wednesday's out for me. I forgot to tell you. I'm going away for a couple of days next week.'

'You *forgot*?' he repeated wrathfully. 'Where are you going?'

She hesitated. 'Jake. It's early. Want some coffee?'

His eyes gleamed. 'You're asking me in?'

'Yes. Are you coming?'

'What do you think?' Jake slid out of the car at top speed, sprinted round it to let her out, then hustled her across the pavement to her door.

'Why the rush?' demanded Sarah, laughing as she put her key in the lock.

'In case you change your mind on the way!'

Margaret Parker emerged from the kitchen as Jake hurried Sarah into the hall.

'Hello, Grandma,' said Sarah blithely. 'This is Jake Hogan. Jake, meet my grandmother, Margaret Parker.'

'Good evening, Mr Hogan,' said Margaret formally.

Jake smiled and held out his hand. 'How do you do, Mrs Parker?'

Margaret took the hand briefly, and even managed a smile. 'How was *A Doll's House*?'

'The understudy had to go on as Nora, and she just

wasn't up to it,' said Sarah, making a face. 'Good thing you decided to give it a miss this week.'

'I'm no Ibsen fan. By the way, I'm afraid you caught me raiding your kitchen, Sarah. I was out of coffee.'

'Come and have some with us,' offered Sarah, but Margaret declined politely, told Jake she'd been pleased to meet him, then took herself back up to her own quarters.

'I see where you get the tortoiseshell eyes,' commented Jake, watching Sarah as she put out cups.

'My mother had them, too. The distaff genes dominate the looks in my family.' Thank God, thought Sarah, as they went into the sitting room.

'Not a night for sitting outside,' she said with regret. 'Last week it was too hot to breathe; this week it's cold enough for autumn.'

'Never mind our famous climate,' said Jake, putting the tray down. 'Tell me where you're going next week.'

'To a wedding.'

'Whose?'

'Old college friend.' She shrugged. 'I must make the effort to go, because Nick's a good friend. And some of my old college crowd will be there—'

'Do I hear a but?' asked Jake.

Sarah nodded. 'The wedding's midweek, which means no problem with Davy, and I had time owing to me at work—I even bought a suitable dress the other day.'

Jake eyed her face as she poured coffee. 'So what's the snag?'

'Pretty feeble, really.' She pulled a face. 'I'll be the only one on my own. The others come in pairs.'

'And you mind that?'

'I do, rather. At this kind of wedding in the past I

always had Nick for company. But this time he's the bridegroom, so I'll be a spare wheel.'

'Does your invitation include a partner?'

'Yes.' She smiled wryly. 'Nick put a note with the invitation, telling me to bring my current man with me.'

Jake gave her one of the direct looks she was coming to know. 'Then why don't you?'

Sarah's eyes widened. 'Are you saying *you* would come with me?'

'Remember I told you I'm strictly a one at a time kind of guy?' said Jake elliptically.

'Yes. Why?'

'I assume you function on the same principle?'

'Of course I do.'

'Then as far as I'm concerned we're a couple.' He gave her a mocking little bow. 'If you want a partner for the occasion, I'm yours. I even own a morning coat.'

Sarah gazed at him, her mind working overtime. The offer was tempting. Very tempting. 'I'm staying overnight,' she warned.

'I'll book a room at the same hotel, then.'

'But can you just take off like that—from Pentiles, I mean?'

'The firm won't grind to a halt if I'm away for a day or two,' he said, then gave her a smile tinged with arrogance. 'I *am* Pentiles, remember. I take time off when I want.'

Sarah frowned. 'If you do come with me,' she began, choosing her words with care, 'my friends will probably read more into it than you'd like.'

'Than *you'd* like,' he corrected. 'I don't see a problem. Just introduce me as a friend.'

'The female section of the group will take one look at you and flatly refuse to believe that!'

Jake frowned. 'Why?'

'You know perfectly well why,' she retorted irritably. One look at those dark-rimmed blue eyes and gold-streaked hair, plus the physique that went with them, and she'd probably be beating girlfriends off with a stick.

'But it's true. I am your friend,' he pointed out. 'Not entirely by choice, on my part, I admit. I'd like a closer relationship. Much closer. But I know damn well I must toe the line or you'll send me packing.' His eyes glittered with sudden heat. 'Sometimes I can't believe I've been tamed so easily.'

Sarah gave him a fulminating look. Jake Hogan might be lounging at ease on her sofa, but with that particular light in his eye he looked about as tame as the average free-range lion.

'If you do come to the wedding—' she began, but he held up a hand.

'I *am* coming. I like weddings.'

'You must be the only man I know who does!'

'As I keep telling you, I'm not the average male,' he reminded her affably. 'And on the subject of weddings I speak from experience, having survived the nuptials of two sisters and several cousins, featured as best man at two of them, and still lived to tell the tale.'

Against her will Sarah began to laugh. 'Oh, all right. Then thank you, Jake. You win.'

'I always do.' He grinned at her. 'So where's the wedding?'

Sarah wasn't in the least surprised to learn that Jake knew the area she mentioned. She listened, amused, while he spoke at persuasive length, first to the receptionist at the Greenacres Hotel in Norfolk, then to the manager, turning on the charm to an outrageous degree before giving his credit card details to secure a room.

'Only one in the place, due to the wedding. The manager was reluctant at first to let me have it, because it's a brand-new renovation and isn't quite finished. But I persuaded her to have it ready by the time I need it,' he said afterwards, and gave Sarah a smile of such blatant triumph she laughed in his face.

'You were shameless. I suppose a technique like that wins for you every time,' she said severely, but he shook his head, sighing.

'Not quite. If I thought it did I'd try it with you, Sarah.' He looked at his watch. 'Time I was off.'

'Look, Jake, if you change your mind,' she said awkwardly. 'About the wedding, I mean, please feel free to do so.'

Jake got up, pulled her to her feet and took her by the shoulders, his eyes utterly serious. 'I won't change my mind. If it makes life easier for you to have a partner at this wedding I'll be there for you, Sarah. We're friends, remember. That's what friends are for.'

Impulsively she reached up to kiss his cheek. 'Thank you, Jake.'

He stepped back, a pulse throbbing visibly at the corner of his mouth. 'Don't mention it,' he said huskily. 'Goodnight, Sarah.'

She walked with him to the door and held up her face for their customary friendly kiss, but he pulled her into his arms and kissed her with such heat and hunger she was speechless when he let her go.

'I'll ring you.' He smiled crookedly into her dazed eyes, then went out to the car and to her intense disappointment drove off, with no mention of meeting again before their trip to Norfolk.

CHAPTER SIX

SARAH was too busy to miss Jake over the weekend. At least, not as much as she'd expected. From the moment she collected Davy and Polly from school life was so hectic her only respite was in bed. There was a picnic tea in the garden when they got home on the Friday afternoon, and a trip to McDonald's later. Once the children were in bed in Davy's room Sarah finished off the work she'd brought home, then fell into bed herself to get some rest in preparation for next day.

The two little girls were up early, Davy eager to introduce the excited Polly to their Saturday programme of swimming, lunch, and cinema. After the film Sarah drove them home to play in the garden before supper, then finished off the day with a round of board games. Margaret surprised Sarah no end by joining in to make up a four.

'Thank you,' said Sarah gratefully, after she'd packed the lively pair off to bed. 'I thought you were going out tonight.'

'I had lunch with Barbara today, instead of our usual supper. We went over arrangements for the Tuscany trip.' Margaret eyed her granddaughter searchingly. 'Sarah, purely as a matter of interest, how does Jake Hogan feel about your no-weekend rule?'

'If he objects he's not saying so. Besides, I laid my cards on the table about Davy from the first. Most of them, anyway,' she added with a sigh, then eyed her grandmother warily. 'By the way, Jake's going to Nick's wedding with me.'

'*Really?*' Dark eyebrows shot to meet the hair that was still as brown as Sarah's under its frosting of silver. 'In what capacity, exactly?'

'As my friend.'

Margaret said nothing for a moment, then gave Sarah a searching look. 'Is that all he is?'

'Of course.' Sarah met the look head-on. 'That's all he can be.'

Sunday morning was fine, with a forecast promising sunshine which augured well for the Rogers' barbecue. After packing Davy's bag for the school week, Sarah wandered round the garden in her dressing gown for a while to gauge the temperature, then went into her room to change into a raspberry linen skirt. She added a plain white shirt, rolled the sleeves to just below her elbows, then went to collect the girls.

'Ready for the off?' said Margaret, on her way downstairs to say goodbye to Davy.

'Yes. Though I'm not sure about the skirt. I'm not exactly up on what the well-dressed barbecue guest is wearing this season.' Sarah made a face. 'I'll feel very silly if everyone else is in jeans.'

But when she delivered Polly to her parents Sarah was relieved to find that only Don was in jeans. Alison was wearing a strappy cotton dress.

'Have you been good?' Alison asked, hugging her daughter, who at top speed proceeded to itemise all the fab things she'd done in Pennington, then rushed Davy into the garden to play.

'I hope you're not worn out, Sarah,' said Don. 'Sit down, have a drink, and relax.'

Sarah took the reclining chair he offered, and assured her hosts that Polly had been no trouble at all over the weekend. 'As you said, it's easier with two. Though I'm afraid they didn't get to sleep very early.'

'They will tonight, back in school,' said Alison comfortably. 'In the meantime thank heavens we're lucky with the weather. Let's just sit for a minute and enjoy the sun. The others aren't due for a while.'

Sarah found it very pleasant to relax for a while in the Rogers' friendly company. When the guests arrived she was introduced to Ned and Helen Fenwick from next door, followed by three more couples from the neighbourhood, and found she was quickly absorbed into the friendly, animated group. When some of the men gave Don a hand with the chicken and steaks he was cooking, or topped up drinks, Alison enlisted Sarah's help in transferring the rest of the food from the house to the trestle table laid under the shade of the sheltering fruit trees.

Glad to be of use, and well aware that Alison's plea for help was to make her feel part of the scene, Sarah hurried to and fro with salads and relishes and baskets of bread. When everything was ready she ducked into the cloakroom to tidy up, then heard the doorbell ring and went out into the hall to let in a belated guest. And stared, speechless, at the sight of Jake Hogan, grinning at her in outrageous triumph, dressed in faded jeans and a shirt which matched his eyes.

'Jake!' called Alison, coming into the hall. 'Long time no see. Hurry up, you're late. Have you met Sarah Tracy?'

'I certainly have,' he said, thrusting a bag of bottles into Alison's arms before kissing her on both cheeks. 'How are you, Ally?'

'A lot older than when I saw you last,' she said, laughing. 'Thank you for these, you extravagant man. Come and have something to drink, then we can eat. Don's been hovering over that barbecue so long he must be medium rare himself by now.'

When Alison hurried back to her guests Jake took Sarah's arm to delay her. 'Are you glad to see me?'

She eyed him accusingly. 'You didn't tell me you were coming.'

'Don didn't invite me until Friday.'

'Rather a coincidence!'

'Not exactly. I just made it my business to contact Don over the phone on Friday. I mentioned I hadn't seen Alison for ages, and that was it.'

Sarah gave him what was meant to be a severe look. 'You didn't think to give me a ring and tell me?'

'I wanted to surprise you.' Jake took her hand. 'Tell me you're pleased, Sarah.'

'I am,' she said, relenting. 'Very pleased.'

'Good.' He gave her the eye-crinkling smile which turned her bones to jelly. 'Where's Davy?'

'Out in the garden with Polly.'

'Will she object to my presence?'

'She's having too good a time to object to anything, so come on; we'd better join the others.'

Sarah had been enjoying herself well enough up to that point, but now Jake Hogan was one of the guests her party spirit soared to the point of euphoria. He accepted a beer and did the round of introductions, then perched himself on the footrest of Sarah's recliner.

When Helen Fenwick asked if anyone had been to the Playhouse that week Jake surprised Alison by saying that he'd taken Sarah there.

'I didn't know you two knew each other so well,' she said, surprised.

'Didn't you?' said Jake blandly. 'How's Polly?'

'Getting filthy in the garden with Sarah's little girl— oh, heavens, what now?' Alison jumped up in alarm as her daughter came tearing across the lawn in distress.

'Davy's stuck up a tree, Sarah, and can't get down,' Polly wailed.

In one fluent move Jake leapt up, pulled Sarah to her feet, and ran with her after Polly.

'You see to the meat, darling.' Don tossed his utensils to Alison, and took off after the others at top speed. 'Is she in one of the oak trees, Polly?' he panted, catching up with his daughter.

'Yes, Daddy. And she's *bleeding*!'

Sarah blenched when they found Davy high above the ground, clinging to a branch of one of the trees edging the Rogers' property.

'Hi, Davy,' said Jake breathlessly as they reached her. 'How did you get up there?'

Davy peered down at him in surprise. 'Hello, Mr Hogan,' she shouted, then her voice quavered. 'It was easy-peasy getting up, but now I'm stuck. I can't get down.'

'Did you hurt yourself?' called Sarah, determinedly calm.

'Only a bit. I scraped my knee.'

Don Rogers, who was a lot heavier than Jake, opted to station himself at the foot of the tree as catcher, leaving Jake to work his way up steadily from branch to branch. When Jake reached a fork in the tree below the frightened child he smiled at her in reassurance and stretched up an arm. 'Right then, Davy. Give me your hand.'

'I can't let go,' she gasped.

'Yes, you can, sweetheart. Just one hand. You can still hang on with the other.'

Sarah watched, heart in her throat, while Davy, apparently reassured by something in the smiling blue eyes trained on hers, fearfully detached one hand and put it into Jake's.

'Good girl!' Don called.

'Now, lean down a little bit and put the other one round my neck,' instructed Jake.

Polly clutched Sarah's hand as with agonising slowness Davy detached her hand and slid her arm round Jake's neck to let him take her weight.

'Well done,' he said, holding her securely. 'Now we're going to climb down a bit.'

'And then Jake is going to hand you down to me,' called Don, smiling up at Davy. 'Just like pass the parcel.'

'OK,' she said bravely, and clung to Jake like a limpet while he made it down to a secure foothold before lowering her into the waiting arms below.

'Here's Mummy to inspect your wounds,' said Don, and gave Davy a kiss. 'And now I must get back to my labours or our lunch will be cinders.'

Polly rushed to inspect the wound, but Davy assured her airily that it was just a scratch, then to Sarah's pride turned to Jake with a beaming smile of gratitude. 'Thank you very much for getting me down, Mr Hogan.'

He grinned as he ruffled her hair. 'Any time, Davy. Glad to be of service.'

'Now, let's go and tell Alison you're in one piece and apologise for holding up lunch,' said Sarah.

Later she took the freshly scrubbed girls to join the

others at the long trestle table, and found Don taking sly pleasure in lauding Jake as the hero of the hour.

'Maidens in distress a specialty,' Jake said flippantly.

'All ages?' called Alison from the foot of the table, to general laughter.

'Absolutely,' he said with a grin, holding Sarah's chair for her.

With Davy safe and sound Sarah settled down to enjoy the party. The food was delicious, and tasted even better for being eaten in the open air in convivial company, and to add to her pleasure Davy, seated the other side of Jake, spent most of the meal chattering happily to him.

The company gathered round the table enjoyed themselves so much that when people finally began to leave it was almost time for Davy and Polly to go back to school.

'I'll take Polly with us,' offered Sarah, as Alison went inside with her to collect her child's belongings together. 'I'm sure you two could do with a breather after working so hard over lunch.'

'Are you sure?' said Alison, obviously tempted.

'It seems pretty pointless for both of us to make the same journey.'

'Or we could take Davy with us?'

'I'd rather do that myself, and explain to her house mother that she had a bit of a fright up the tree.' Sarah smiled sheepishly. 'I'm fussing, I know—'

'Of course you're not fussing,' said Alison, and gave Sarah a knowing little smile. 'By the way, I didn't know Jake Hogan was a friend of yours.'

'Small world,' said Sarah casually. 'Now, we'd better get those two out of the bath.'

When the two girls ran downstairs, transformed from

grubby hoydens into neat little schoolgirls, Jake was still chatting in the garden with Don.

'Hey, look at you two,' he said, jumping up. 'Who waved a magic wand?'

Alison laughed, and looked at her watch. 'There's time, yet, Sarah. Have some tea before you go. And you two sit quietly and don't get dirty, please.'

Sarah was only too pleased to stay on a while, but deep down couldn't help feeling wistful. To the onlooker the four of them looked so much like two conventional couples with a child apiece she was pierced with a stab of longing for the impossible.

After Alison took Don into the house with her, apparently in need of his help to make a pot of tea, Jake moved his chair closer to Sarah's.

'Have you recovered from the drama with Davy?' he asked quietly.

'I'm used to it. She has a real thing about trees, but she never learns. At one time or another she's been stuck up every one of ours in the garden at Campden Road,' Sarah told him, her eyes on the girls as they sat on a rug on the grass, playing some absorbing private game.

'But other than that you've had a good time today?'

Sarah turned to look at him, her eyes luminous. 'Better than good. I've never been to anything like this before.'

Jake frowned in surprise. 'Why not?'

'It doesn't take rocket science to work that one out, Jake.' She shrugged. 'All the people here today were couples.'

'You don't get invited to parties?'

'Some. Colleagues' birthdays, Christmas drinks with the families of the men I work for, the odd charity bash. Which is how I met Brian. But no family affairs like this.' Sarah straightened in her chair. 'I'm whingeing. Sorry.'

'Don asked if we were seeing each other,' said Jake casually.

Sarah frowned. 'What did you say?'

'The truth. Because we are seeing each other. Literally.' He heaved a dramatic sigh. 'My ego wasn't up to admitting that ours was a no-kisses type of romance.'

She flushed. 'I wouldn't say no kisses at all.'

'Next best thing,' he whispered, as Don came back hefting a tray.

Much as Sarah would have liked the day to go for ever, shortly afterwards it was time to see her young passengers into the car and say her goodbyes. 'We've had such a good time,' she told her hosts.

'Come again soon,' said Don genially, and cocked an eyebrow at Jake. 'Both of you.'

'Dinner next time,' said Alison, nodding. 'Then we'll have more time to talk.'

'I'll ring you, Sarah,' said Jake, and she gave him a quick, embarrassed smile, conscious of the interest from the other two. Jake popped his head inside the open window at the back of the car. 'Mind you keep out of trees, Davy. You too, Polly.'

The giggling children promised, waved at Alison and Don, and Sarah drove off to a chorus of goodbyes. When she got to Roedale Sarah had a quick word with the house mother to give the reason for Davy's grazed knee, gave both girls a hug and drove back to Pennington, anticlimax creeping up on her, stronger with every mile. Her Sunday evening blues were back in force. But not for the usual reason.

When she'd parked the car in the garage at the bottom

of the garden, Sarah wandered aimlessly up the path, rounded the shrubbery and felt a leap of unadulterated joy at the sight of Jake sitting at the patio table, reading the Sunday papers.

He jumped up as she approached, smiling rather warily. 'Mrs Parker let me in. Do you mind?'

'Of course I don't,' said Sarah, so obviously meaning it his eyes lit up in response as she sat down in one of the chairs at the table. 'Second surprise of the day.'

'I wanted to see you alone,' he said matter-of-factly, and drew a chair up close beside her.

'Why didn't you say so earlier?'

'Originally you said you'd be too tired. So I thought you'd say no. And we need to make arrangements for the wedding.'

'You could have rung me.'

'I could,' he agreed. 'But I like this much better.' He looked at her steadily. 'So I rang your grandmother's bell. She was on her way out to church, so I offered to wait in the car until you got back from Roedale, but she suggested I wait in the garden instead.'

'I'm glad she did. It's a very *nice* surprise,' she said after a while, her eyes falling.

'For once I could tell,' he said dryly. 'Normally you don't give much away, Sarah Tracy.'

'I'm not the effusive type. Want a drink?' she asked.

'Not really. I just want to sit here with you in the cool of the evening and talk, or not talk, as the case may be. I enjoyed the day so much I wanted it to last longer.'

'So did I,' she confessed.

'Good.' Jake stretched out his long legs with a sigh. 'Have you remembered that I'm in London tomorrow? I'll be back at the grind on Tuesday afternoon, but I'll work late so I can take off for Norfolk with a clear conscience.'

'Look,' said Sarah quickly, 'if the trip is causing problems for you—'

'It isn't.' He turned to smile at her. 'As I keep telling you, I like weddings.'

'As long as you're not the bridegroom, I suppose!'

'Not a bit of it. Come the day, I'll enjoy my own wedding most of all,' he assured her, and held her eyes with the intensity which always braced her for what was coming next. 'Did you never consider getting married, Sarah?'

'No,' she said, after a taut little silence. 'Never.'

'Not even to Davy's father?'

'Him least of all.'

'And you obviously don't want to talk about it,' he said after a moment, and turned his attention back to the sunset. 'Right. So what time shall I come for you on Wednesday?'

'Early, I'm afraid. The wedding's not until three, but it's a fair trip, and I'll need time when we arrive to tidy up and change into my finery. Which reminds me,' she added. 'Do you possess a golf umbrella?'

He grinned. 'No. But I can borrow one. Why?'

'So we can arrive in church in reasonable nick if it rains, of course.'

'I'll see to it,' he promised.

While the shadows lengthened, and the sun disappeared over the trees at the end of the garden, they went on talking with the easy familiarity of friends of a lot longer standing than they actually were, at peace with the world and each other.

'I've enjoyed today,' said Jake at one stage, and shot

a look at Sarah. 'I didn't spoil things for you by gate-crashing the party?'

'Not in the least.' Finding it easier to admit in the fading light, Sarah told him the truth. 'I was delighted to see you, Jake.'

'Thank God for that. But you realise that Don and Alison now have us pigeonholed as a couple?' he added.

'Next time I see them I'll tell them we're not,' she said, unconcerned.

'Why?' Jake demanded. 'Maybe we're not exactly the sort of couple they think we are. But we're definitely a pair of some kind, Sarah.'

'If the subject comes up I'll say we're just good friends.'

'Which will convince them beyond all doubt that we're lovers.' Jake heaved a sigh. 'Which we're not, alas.'

Sarah shivered suddenly, and rubbed her arms. 'It's getting chilly. Let's go inside. I'll make some supper.'

Switching lights on as she went, Sarah led the way to the kitchen. 'How do you feel about omelettes?'

'Enthusiastic,' he assured her. 'Though I didn't come here tonight expecting to be fed.'

'What exactly did you expect?'

Jake's smile was wry. 'Very little, Miss Tracy. A habit I'm learning fast where you're concerned, to avoid disappointment. Can I do something?'

'No.' She flashed a gleaming dark look at him. 'Just sit there and look decorative while I work.'

He threw back his head and laughed.

The kitchen, which had originally served the entire household, was now Sarah's private domain. But years before it had been renovated to Margaret Parker's requirements, with modern appliances and cupboards, and plenty of space for pots of herbs on the broad ledge of a window Sarah's master builder grandfather had en- larged to give his wife a better view of the garden. These days Margaret's state-of-the art kitchen was upstairs in her self-contained flat, converted from a small spare bed- room with the same view.

When they sat down to eat puffy omelettes flavoured with parsley and chives, Jake attacked his with gusto.

'Though after the lunch we ate I hadn't expected to be hungry again today,' he commented.

Sarah glanced up at the clock on the wall. 'It's after nine. Hours since lunch. Have some more bread.'

'This is a big kitchen for just you, Sarah,' he said, eyeing his surroundings.

'Especially as my main activity in here is throwing a salad together! But in its heyday it would have served a big household, probably as much as a dozen or so orig- inally.' She smiled. 'Three attic bedrooms and four dou- ble bedrooms, one with dressing room. But originally only one bathroom—with a solitary lavatory inside it— to serve all the occupants. At one time there was another, in an outhouse at the back, but that was kept for the servants' use, in the days when people had such things.'

Jake smiled. 'Sounds like the setting for a television costume drama.'

Sarah got up to take their plates, then made coffee. 'It's a huge contrast to the home I grew up in. My father was a civil engineer who worked in hotel construction all over the world. He had a house built for my mother, complete with every gadget and convenience possible to make life easy for her.'

'Was your mother delicate, then?'

'She wasn't the most robust of people, it's true, but that wasn't the reason. It was just the way Dad was with her. Always.' Sarah leaned against the counter, waiting for the coffee to perk. 'I only realised how special their marriage was when I was old enough to notice other people's. My parents idolised each other.'

Jake looked at her questioningly. 'Did that mean you felt excluded?'

'Good heavens, no. I felt part of the equation, always.' She brought the coffee pot over and sat down to pour.

He leaned over to touch her hand. 'So there was no problem with them when Davy was born?'

Sarah kept her eyes on her task. 'Not in that way.'

Jake leaned back again. 'But it must have been pretty tough for a teenager, just the same.'

'Not nearly as tough as for some. Because Davy was born in my gap year I was able to take up my college place, as planned. And I led a normal, rackety student life during term, but switched back to the role of Mummy when I went home—' Sarah stopped abruptly. 'This isn't something I normally discuss, Jake.'

'I'm very much aware of that. Thank you, Sarah. And now,' he added briskly, 'what time shall I call for you on Wednesday morning?'

'I'd like to get there by twelve if possible,' she said, grateful to him for changing the subject.

'Right. I'll be here at six.'

'Sorry to get you up at that hour.'

'Not a bit of it. I wake early most mornings,' he assured her. 'And I'd rather start when the roads are relatively quiet. We can stop for coffee somewhere, to break the journey, and grab something to eat at the hotel when we get there.'

Sarah smiled at him gratefully. 'This is very good of you, Jake.'

'As I keep saying, Miss Tracy, it's what friends are

for.' He got up reluctantly. 'Thank you for supper. Shall I help wash up?'

She shook her head, laughing. 'You're just too good to be true, Jake Hogan. I'll let you off the dishes in case your halo gets too tight.'

He grinned. 'I only offered so I could stay longer!'

'You can do that anyway. Come back to the sitting room for a while.'

He followed her into the other room and sat down with her on the sofa. 'Good. Now we can practise behaving like the old friends we're supposed to be. Though that isn't difficult. Not for me, anyway.'

'Nor for me.' Sarah turned her head on the sofa-back to look at him. 'I'm very glad you came to the lunch today, Jake.'

'So am I.' He smiled into her eyes. 'I'll send flowers to Alison tomorrow. Though she won't know I'm really thanking her for an entire Sunday spent with you. Not something that's likely to occur often, alas.'

'True,' Sarah agreed with regret.

'Would Davy really object if the three of us spent time together?'

'Probably not. But that isn't going to happen just the same, Jake.'

He was silent for a moment. 'Why not?'

She sighed. 'Because you and I may not remain— friends, Jake. So I can't risk any attachment to you on Davy's part. Her world fell apart when my parents died. It's taken from that time almost until now to give her any real sense of security. This wavered badly when she went to board at Roedale, but she's getting back on course again now and I want her to stay that way.'

Jake looked across at the photograph of the two smiling faces, then turned back to Sarah. 'So are you saying you've never had a relationship since Davy was born?'

'No, I'm not. I had boyfriends in college, like everyone else, but nothing significant. And Davy was never involved.' Sarah looked away. 'I led a perfectly normal life—or what I thought of as a normal life—until my parents died. After that everything changed. We had to move in here with my grandmother, and you know the rest.'

'So you won't let a man into your life in case the relationship harms Davy,' said Jake slowly.

'Which has been no problem up to now,' she admitted.

Jake reached out a hand to turn her face to his. 'Up to now,' he repeated inexorably. 'Does that mean you'd consider a closer relationship with me if it weren't for Davy?'

Sarah nodded wordlessly, then closed her eyes, suddenly defenceless when he drew her into his arms. 'Please, Jake!'

'Please what?' he whispered, and kissed her very gently.

It wasn't fair, she thought wildly. The merest touch of Jake's lips roused all kinds of hot, unbidden responses never experienced with the most passionate overtures from anyone else.

'Don't push me away, Sarah. You need a little tender loving care,' he whispered, raising his head a fraction.

'Is that what this is?' she said unevenly, and closed her eyes against the heat in his.

'Yes,' he said tightly. 'And it's killing me, because I want a hell of a lot more.'

He kissed her again, and this time the kiss was hot and hard, and for the first time she answered it in kind, shivers running down her spine as his tongue met hers and his hands slid upwards beneath her shirt to caress her bare back. Her breasts tautened in anticipation of the caresses she was sure would happen any second as the kiss deepened. The growing hunger of it set her body alight, and she gasped as his fingers sought the nipples straining against the thin cotton of her shirt. Heat streaked through her from his fingertips, the shock of it causing such turbulence her inevitable defence mechanism sprang to life, and she jerked away violently, hands outstretched to ward him off.

Jake gave a smothered groan and leapt to his feet to stand at the windows, his chest heaving as he stared out blindly into the dark, while Sarah slumped into a corner of the sofa, feeling as though she'd been dropped from a great height. It was a long time before she could trust her voice, but at last she cleared her throat, her dark eyes heavy with remorse. 'I'm sorry, Jake.'

He stayed where he was, his back turned to her. 'So am I,' he said tersely. 'Because you're a puzzle I just can't solve. I want you, Sarah. And it hurts like hell to know you don't want me.'

'Ah, but I do,' she said miserably.

Jake turned sharply, his eyes blazing into hers. 'So why—?' Colour leached suddenly from his face. 'Sarah, for God's sake, tell me! Were you raped?'

Sarah jumped up to take his hands. '*No*, Jake. It was nothing like that.'

Jake held her close, his cheek rubbing against her hair as he let out a deep breath of relief. 'Thank goodness for that, at least.' He pulled away a little and smiled down at her. 'Maybe one day you'll be able to tell me about it. When you know me better. Which I'm determined you will. Better than anyone else in the world, in fact. But for now I'm going to let you get some rest and take myself off home.'

'Thank you, Jake,' she said huskily.

'What for, exactly?'

Sarah's eyes were luminous in her flushed face. 'Everything.'

CHAPTER SEVEN

MARGARET PARKER left for Pisa with a group of friends next day. And without her formidable presence the atmosphere in the house seemed lighter. Far from feeling lonely or nervous, Sarah was happy to have the place to herself, her spirits rising even further when Jake rang.

'Just thought I'd report in, check that all was well with you, Sarah.'

'How nice of you.'

'I *am* nice.' He chuckled. 'My day has been incredibly boring, so tell me about yours.'

'Much the same as usual, except for a shopping spree after work. And I've been chatting to Nick, the amazingly jittery bridegroom. He rang earlier to make sure I was coming.'

'Did you mention me?'

'I certainly did. He told me to say he's looking forward to meeting you, then went on at enormous length about the virtues of his Delphine. The man's head over heels in love at last!'

'You don't mind that?'

'Of course not. Nick and I have always been the best of friends. But there was never anything else between us.'

'So I've no reason to feel jealous?'

'None at all.' Sarah paused. '*Are* you the jealous type, Jake?'

'Only when you're concerned, it seems,' he said lightly. 'So tell me about your shopping spree.'

'I hired a hat for the occasion.'

'One of those big cartwheel affairs?'

'No. Small and frivolous.'

'Can't wait to see you in it. What else did you buy?'

'The wedding gift—'

'I'm glad you mentioned that. As well as the pleasure of talking to you, Miss Tracy, I rang to pick your brains. What shall *I* buy the happy pair?'

'Since you've never met them, you don't need to buy them anything.'

'What did you choose?'

Sarah described the hand-carved wooden fruit bowl she'd chosen, but glossed over the fact that its price tag had put paid to new shoes. 'We can both sign the card,' she suggested.

'Then I insist on paying half—I won't ruffle your feathers by offering to foot the entire bill!'

'Wise man,' she said, laughing. 'Half will do nicely.' So nicely she might search through the sales for shoes next day after all.

'I'll be home latish tomorrow evening, Sarah, but I'll be with you bright and early on Wednesday.'

'I'll be ready. Goodnight, Jake. Thanks for ringing.'

'My pleasure.'

Her pleasure too, Sarah acknowledged as she got ready for bed. Added to the sexual attraction which grew stronger every time they met, she liked every last thing about Jake Hogan. His smile, his voice, his looks. His touch. The mere thought of his hands on her skin and his mouth on hers, and— Her mind veered away sharply. She knew she was a frustrating puzzle to Jake, but there were some vital missing pieces to put in place before she could even begin to consider the kind of relationship he wanted. And which she was beginning to want just as much.

Sarah was in the middle of packing the following evening when Jake rang her doorbell, demanding entry.

She let him in, her delight undisguised at the sight of him. Then her eyes widened in dismay. Something had happened. He couldn't take her to the wedding after all. 'Something wrong, Jake?'

'I just needed to see you,' he said simply, and kissed her briefly.

Sarah was so pleased to hear it she kissed him back. 'I thought you'd come to say you couldn't make it tomorrow,' she said, as they went into the sitting room.

'Not a bit of it,' he assured her, and sank down on the sofa, stifling a yawn. 'I've spent the last two days working my socks off to make sure I can leave Pentiles to its own devices for a while.'

'Have you eaten?'

'Yes. I took pity on my staff and had something sent in between meetings. So right now I just want to sit and hold hands with you for a few minutes.' Jake held up his hand and Sarah took it, letting him draw her down beside him.

'You look tired,' she commented.

'I am. But I shall get myself to bed early tonight. And then tomorrow I'm yours,' he assured her. 'All through the meetings and presentations I missed you yesterday, Sarah. I missed you today, too. Which is why I'm here, even though I'll be seeing you in the morning.' His grasp tightened. 'And not just for the kiss—which I couldn't help when I saw the worried look in those beautiful eyes.'

'Worried I didn't have a driver for tomorrow,' she agreed with feeling.

He moved closer. 'Would you have been disappointed?'

'Yes.' Sarah looked down at their clasped hands. 'And not just because I didn't want to go alone, either.'

Jake put a finger under her chin to turn her face up to his. 'Can it be the lady's warming towards me?'

'You know I am!' She met his eyes steadily. 'But the situation still stands, Jake.'

He nodded, resigned. 'But the odd friendly kiss can't do any harm. In fact,' he added, melting her with the eye-crinkling smile, 'it would do me a whole lot of good.'

For answer she tilted her chin in invitation.

Jake kissed her gently, then took her by surprise by lifting her onto his lap. When she leaned into him instead of struggling to get away he gave a relishing sigh and held her close. But after a moment or two his arms tightened, and heat flared in his eyes, the pupils extending to cover the blue iris. Sarah gazed into them, spellbound, and with a smothered sound he bent his head and kissed her, his tongue caressing hers. She melted against him, responding with such fervour their hearts were thudding in unison when the need for air forced them to separate. Breathing hard, Jake straightened with reluctance and gazed down into her dazed face.

'I was wrong. That did me no good at all.'

'I know what you mean,' she said unevenly. 'If those are your friendly kisses what are the passionate ones like? Don't demonstrate!' she added hastily, then frowned. 'That's an unsettling look in your eye. What's wrong?'

Jake was silent for a moment, then gave her an oddly bleak smile. 'I keep wondering about your old pal Nick

Morrell.' He gave her a hard, devouring kiss by way of illustration. 'Were you on these kind of terms with him?'

Sarah shook her head vehemently. 'No. Not like this. Never like this. With anyone.'

'No one at all?' Jake smoothed the hair away from her forehead, his eyes holding hers.

'I know what you're asking, Jake.' She would have slid from his lap, but he held her fast. 'All right. I'll tell you just one thing, Jake, on condition we don't talk about it any more.' She sat rigid for a moment, then sagged against him, burying her face against his shoulder. 'Other than my grandmother, no one knows that Davy owes her existence to a single moment of misguided sympathy.'

Jake stroked her hair in silence for a moment, then stood up with her and set her on her feet. 'Thank you, darling. It can't have been easy for you to tell me that. And now I must go. See you in the morning.'

'You were right, Jake. You are definitely not the average male.' Sarah smiled crookedly. 'Any other man would be hammering at me with more questions.'

He kissed her again. 'I admit I want to know every last thing about you, Sarah, but I promise I'll be patient until you can trust me with the entire story. So get some sleep, darling. It's going to be a long day tomorrow.'

Jake arrived next morning on the stroke of six, as promised, in jeans and a navy jersey over a thin shirt, which was so similar to Sarah's choice of clothes she laughed as he gave her a swift kiss.

'We look like twins,' she told him.

'Not quite,' he said with a grin, giving her a head-to-toe survey.

Jake refused coffee in favour of leaving immediately

to avoid the morning rush hour, stowed Sarah's belongings in the car, then waited while she made sure the house was secure.

'My grandmother's on holiday,' she explained, sliding into the passenger seat. 'But I've plugged in the gadgets that make the lights come on, and cancelled the milk and newspapers, and double-checked all the windows and doors.'

'Then you were alone in the house last night?' asked Jake as he drove off.

'Yes.'

He slanted a look at her. 'But you didn't tell me that in case I carried you up to your bed and demanded my evil way, I suppose?'

'I sleep downstairs, so it doesn't apply,' she said, unmoved. 'And, believe it or not, I just forgot to mention it.'

'I believe everything you tell me, Sarah.'

'Good. Anyway, it was Grandma's trip to Italy which originally gave me doubts about going to the wedding. But the school has my mobile number, and the details of the hotel in Norfolk, and Alison offered to stand in as back-up for Davy if the need arises.' Sarah shivered. 'Which I devoutly hope it won't.'

Jake touched her hand for an instant. 'Of course it won't. But even if it does I'll get you back here at the speed of light.'

'I hope that's not your normal approach to motorway driving?' she asked, laughing.

'Don't worry, you'll arrive in one piece, but I may need a bit of guidance to find the actual spot once we leave the A11.'

'No problem, I'm a brilliant navigator,' she assured

him. 'But we've got a lot of motorway to get through yet before I start grappling with a map.'

Jake drove not only with speed, but with such skill Sarah relaxed when she found he was capable of paying attention to the road at the same time as giving details of his trip to London, which had included a meal eaten with his brother.

'Did you tell him about me, Jake?'

'Yes.'

Sarah gave him a wry glance. 'Was he surprised? Or didn't you tell him about Davy?'

'Of course I did. We're pretty close, Liam and I. We like to know the other is enjoying life.'

'And is Liam enjoying his?'

'The work part, yes, as usual. But his romance has come unstuck.'

'Poor Liam.' Sarah changed the subject to talk about the wedding, which had put a strain on the accommodation available in the area. 'Nick says the bride's family lives in a vast old rectory, which will be crammed to the rafters with as many relations as possible to leave room in the area for the other guests.'

'Talking of which, how, exactly, do I introduce myself to your chums?' asked Jake.

'As Sarah's friend, of course.'

'A bit lukewarm for my taste. You won't allow lover, I know, and I draw the line at boyfriend. How about partner?'

She shook her head. 'That implies that we live together.'

'As we would, if I had my way,' he said, startling her.

'But how can you want that when we've never even—?' she began, then stopped, colour flooding her face.

'Made love?' He sent her a smouldering look, then returned his attention to the three lanes of motorway crowded as far as the eye could see by this time with London-bound traffic. 'The fact had not escaped my attention, Sarah. Though the foretaste I've been granted makes it obvious we'd be good together. More than good. Sensational.' He drew in a deep breath. 'Now for pity's sake let's change the subject—it's bad for me when I'm driving.'

They stopped later at a motorway service restaurant for coffee and toast and a breather for Jake, who declined Sarah's offer to help with the driving.

'Not,' he assured her, 'because I refuse to let a woman drive me. But I don't want you to arrive at the hotel too tired to enjoy the wedding.'

'Thank you,' she said, her smile so warm Jake reached a hand across the table to take hers.

'Are you aware of the effect of that smile of yours?'

'No,' she said, surprised.

'I thought so. Be sparing with it today. With other men,' he added.

Sarah's eyes flashed. 'Orders, Jake?'

'Advice, not orders.' He wagged an admonishing finger. 'I'm your escort, Miss Tracy, so save that particular smile for me.'

It had been cool with early-morning mist when they started out, but by this time the sun was so hot they discarded their sweaters before resuming their journey.

'"Happy the bride the sun shines on,"' said Sarah.

'It's going to be a scorcher,' agreed Jake, and donned dark glasses for the rest of the journey.

Due to Jake's powerful car, and his skill as a driver, plus the added bonus of Sarah's navigating skills, they arrived at the Greenacres Hotel shortly after eleven.

Sarah spotted the bridegroom in the bar with a trio of friends, and all four of them came rushing to greet her the moment she appeared in the doorway. Grinning broadly, Nick Morrell got there first, and gave her a crushing hug before passing her on to Frances and Grania, then to Paul, completing the circle of friends who had once shared a house with Sarah in student days.

Once the hugging and kissing had abated, Sarah took Jake by the hand and drew him forward. 'This is Jake Hogan, everyone.'

Jake was immediately pounced on by both women, but Nick interrupted, laughing, so he could introduce Paul Bailey, his best man.

'Present company came to provide moral support, to make sure I don't get too nervous to remember my lines. Order more coffee, Paul, would you? The others will be back shortly,' said Nick, putting an arm round Sarah. 'Ben—Grania's husband,' he told Jake, 'is out searching the neighbourhood for a bed for the night.'

'With my Tom as guide, which is worrying, because he's never been to this neck of the woods before,' put in Frances. 'We tried wheedling at the little place we're in, but no luck. Everything's booked solid locally for the wedding.'

'It's all my fault,' said Grania penitently. 'I meant to book the minute I got the invitation, then it went clean out of my mind. By the time I got round to it there was no room at any inn at all.' She pulled a face. 'Ben is not pleased with me. I've grovelled to the receptionist here for first refusal if a cancellation comes in, but that's a pretty fond hope. Never mind. We can always sleep in the car.'

'The men can do that,' said Frances instantly. 'You can bunk in with me.'

Grania shook her head. 'That's sweet of you, Fran, but I wouldn't dream of putting Tom out just because I was an idiot. Anyway, Sarah, let's get on to more important subjects. We want to hear all about your gorgeous Davy—' She halted, casting an uncertain glance at Jake.

'Apart from getting stuck up a tree on Sunday,' he said quickly, 'Davy's doing fine.'

There were instant demands to see photographs, and exclamations over the child's extraordinary likeness to Sarah now she was growing up.

'We all feel a bit proprietary about Davy, Jake,' Nick explained. 'We've known her since she was in her buggy.'

'I envy you that,' said Jake quietly.

'She's a poppet,' said Grania, and smiled proudly. 'Talking of which, guess what, folks?' She paused dramatically. 'We're hoping to achieve something similar ourselves by Christmas!'

The stop-press news brought a flood of congratulations and kisses all round, then Nick looked at his watch and blenched, instantly transformed into panicking bridegroom mode.

'Sorry, must dash. Promised to collect my brother from the station. Coming, Paul? See you all in church.' Looking harassed, he thrust a hand through his dark curly hair, thanked everyone for the gifts, then hurried off with Paul.

'Poor dear,' said Frances, shaking her head. 'I thought women suffered bridal nerves, not laid-back people like Nick.'

'Ben was just the same,' said Grania, and sighed deeply. 'Oh, dear. I hope he comes back with good news.'

'So do I,' said Sarah, then turned to Jake. 'Perhaps we'd better check in.'

'Right. I'll bring the luggage in.' He smiled warmly at Frances and Grania. 'Good to meet you. I'll see you later.'

After he'd gone out to the car Sarah's one-time house-mates pounced on her.

'Does this mean you're going to give Davy a daddy at last?' asked Grania eagerly.

Sarah shook her head, flushing. 'We're just friends.'

'Pull the other one, ducky,' said Frances, laughing. 'The man's obviously nuts about you—and not at all happy to see Nick cuddling you, either.'

'Stop it, Fran,' said Grania, who had always been the one to look out for Sarah most in the past. 'You're making her blush. But Jake's definitely a charmer. Have you known him long?'

'Not very long,' said Sarah, smiling as she saw Jake beckon from the foyer. 'I must dash.'

'I'm famished, as always by this time of day,' said Grania, patting her middle. 'So when you're settled in come back down and have a snack lunch with us, Sarah. Ben and Tom should surely be back by then.'

'Love to. See you later.'

Sarah hurried from the bar to take her hatbox from Jake. 'Could we talk somewhere before checking in?' she muttered in his ear.

'Yes, of course. There's a sofa over there.' He gave her a searching look. 'Sit down. Tell me what's wrong, and what I can do to help.'

She smiled gratefully. 'Jake, what sort of room did you book?'

To her astonishment he looked embarrassed. 'You'll laugh.'

'Of course I won't. Did they put you in the broom closet, or something?'

'Quite the reverse. They let me have the spanking new bridal suite. Not required by your friend and his bride, obviously.' He shrugged. 'It was that or nothing.'

'You're joking! What on earth does it cost?' she said, giggling.

'Don't ask.' He took her hand. 'So tell me, what's your problem, Sarah, and how can I solve it for you?'

She sighed. 'It's just that Grania's pregnant.'

Jake nodded. 'And you're worried at the idea of her sleeping in the car.'

'Exactly. I feel guilty because I booked a double room, and heaven knows what size yours is. It seems so awful not to hand one of them over, but—'

'There's obviously more, so spit it out.'

Sarah looked at him in appeal. 'This sounds stupid, but even if you agree to let me share with you I don't want the world to know we originally booked separate rooms.'

Jake's eyes gleamed. 'Run that past me again. You actually want to share with me?'

'So Grania can have my room, yes,' she said impatiently. 'There must be a sofa I can sleep on?'

'You'd better hope so,' he said, after a pause, 'because any bridal suite worth the name is certain to have a double bed.'

'I realise that. Would you mind sharing with me?'

Jake let out a deep breath, a wry twist to his lips. 'No, Sarah. I wouldn't mind at all. But are you sure about this?'

'Of course I'm sure. So what do we do?'

'Tell the receptionist we double-booked by mistake, and to pass your room on to your friend without mentioning you,' said Jake promptly. 'What's Grania's surname again?'

'Forrester.'

'Right. Wait here.'

Jake crossed the hall to the reception desk, and Sarah looked on, impressed, while the Hogan charm went into overdrive as he explained the apparent mistake. The young woman behind the desk listened with rapt attention, then nodded with enthusiasm, smiling warmly at Jake. She sent an envious, dewy-eyed look in Sarah's direction, and went off towards the bar.

'What on earth did you say?' whispered Sarah, when Jake rejoined her.

'That I'd booked the bridal suite as a special surprise for you, unaware that you'd already made a reservation. And don't worry, I emphasised that you were not only anxious that Mrs Forrester should have yours, but wanted the arrangement kept secret to avoid any embarrassment.'

'What embarrassment?'

'I gave her a mysterious smile and didn't specify. It seemed to go down well.'

'It must have. I think she's already gone to find Grania. Better make ourselves scarce.'

Crammed into the small lift with their luggage, Sarah suddenly broke up with laughter, and Jake sagged against the wall, joining in.

'I would have been hopeless as a spy!' he said, when he could get his breath. 'It was hard to keep a straight face when I was doing my bit with the receptionist.'

'But doing it so *well*,' mocked Sarah, as the doors opened on the top floor.

'Just for you,' he reminded her.

'What's the room number?' she asked, as they went out into a corridor.

'We haven't arrived yet,' said Jake, leading the way past closed doors. 'We foot it the rest of the way, up those stairs at the end.'

Intrigued, Sarah followed him up to a landing, where it was immediately obvious which room was theirs because there was only one door.

'Former attic bedrooms now converted into bridal suite,' said Jake. He put down the bags and unlocked the door.

Sarah went ahead of him into a long, light-filled room, her eyes drawn instantly to a tester bed with filmy white drapes. She looked away quickly, concentrating on the décor instead. 'Well, well,' she said, as Jake closed the door behind him. 'You should feel right at home here.'

'Why?'

'It's like your flat. Pale colours, white bed. Almost minimalist. Not everyone's idea of a bridal suite.'

'Which it isn't tonight,' Jake said with regret.

'True.' Sarah laid her hatbox and garment bag on a narrow settle grouped with a pair of chairs and a table under one of the windows. 'Where do I hang my things?'

Jake went over to a series of brass handles let into one wall and pulled on one to discover a wardrobe. 'And over there,' he added, pointing to a door in the other wall, 'must be the bathroom.'

Because she was the one who'd asked to share Sarah did her best to hide any awkwardness. 'Right,' she said briskly. 'Grania asked us to join them for a snack lunch when we're ready.'

'Good, I'm hungry,' said Jake, unzipping the cover from his morning coat. 'I'll just hang this up, then I'll leave you to sort out your gear. I'll wait for you in the bar.'

Sarah smiled at him with gratitude. 'Thank you, Jake. This is very good of you.'

'A beautiful woman asks to share my room and it's good of me to agree?' Jake shook his head, his eyes gleaming. 'If I *were* good I'd offer to give the room up to you and sleep in the car, Sarah. But I can't see that happening, somehow. Don't be long, and don't forget to bring the key with you,' he added, and left her alone.

Afraid that her solution to Grania's problem was likely to cause quite a few for herself, one way and another, Sarah hung her dress away, pleased to see that it had survived without creasing. She unpacked her bag, then opened the door into the bathroom. And laughed out loud. Mirror-tiled walls reflected opulence the exact opposite of the bedroom's restraint. The interior designer had gone overboard with gold dolphins. They were inlaid in the glass housing the shower, frolicked on the filmy curtains at the window, and accessed water to the sunken circular tub. Several more held up shelves laden with every bathtime luxury a guest could possibly need, and they even bordered fluffy white towels piled on a gilt chair. Everything your average sybarite could possibly want, thought Sarah, amused.

She washed her face, touched it up again, then went back into the bedroom. But no sofa had materialised by magic in the meantime. Not counting the small, decorative settle under the window, and the sunken tub in the bathroom, the only place to sleep was the ineluctably bridal bed.

CHAPTER EIGHT

THERE was an air of celebration in the bar when Sarah joined the others. Tom Hill and Ben Forrester made a great fuss of her, while Grania, euphoric with relief, gave the news that there had been a cancellation after all.

'So Grania won't have to sleep in the car,' Jake said, smiling at Sarah as he seated her beside him.

'Thank God,' said Ben fervently. 'I'm pretty damn relieved myself, I can tell you. We went right through the list we were given, plus a few more places we found on the way, but no luck.' He gave a rueful look at his wife. 'I don't mind telling you, I dreaded breaking the news when I got back.'

'But he didn't have to because miracles do happen sometimes after all,' said Grania, elated. 'I can hardly believe our luck.'

'Is the room comfortable?' said Sarah, avoiding Jake's eye.

'Small and basic, but compared with the alternative it's utter luxury!'

'By the way, Tom, I told Grania you could sleep in the car, and she could share with me if the worst came to the worst,' Frances told her husband, then laughed with everyone else at the comical dismay on his face.

'Of course I'd have done that,' he said loftily, then grinned. 'But I'm bloody glad I don't have to.'

Sarah was happy to be among the friends she rarely saw these days. And it was a double bonus to find that Jake not only blended effortlessly into the group, but had gained much approval for his forethought in ordering pots of coffee and an enormous platter of assorted sandwiches for the lunch everyone needed to eat quickly before going off to change for the wedding.

'Good man,' said Ben fervently, munching. 'I'm famished after knocking on all those doors. Emotionally drained, too,' he added with drama. 'Good thing we're having coffee. A beer would knock me flat.'

'Not that you're allowed one, anyway, with champagne to come later,' said Grania, and smiled warmly at Jake. 'This was such a good idea of yours. Thank you.'

'How long have you known Sarah, Jake?' asked Frances curiously.

'Not long enough,' he assured her.

'How did you meet?'

'He ran me over in his car,' explained Sarah, and grinned at the startled faces turned in her direction. 'You did ask!'

'She gave me the worst fright of my entire life,' said Jake, shuddering.

'Good heavens,' said Grania, awestruck. 'Were you hurt, Sarah?'

'Just a graze or two and a bruised thigh. It was my fault, really. Jake did his utmost to avoid me. I literally shot out into the road in front of him. In the middle of a thunderstorm,' Sarah added, laughing at the instant comprehension on the assembled faces.

'Ah! All is revealed,' Frances told Jake. 'Sarah goes bananas in a storm. In our student days the faintest rumble of thunder sent her diving into the broom cupboard.'

Lunch over, it was decided to make a move and meet in the foyer at two-fifteen for the short drive to the church.

'Tom and I can direct you, needless to say,' said Ben,

grinning. 'After this morning we know every nook and cranny in the entire neighbourhood!'

After Frances and Tom were waved off the others made for the lift.

'Bit of a tight fit,' commented Ben. 'Push up, Sarah. What floor are you on?'

'Right at the top,' said Jake.

'So are we,' said Grania, pleased.

'We're a floor above that again,' Sarah explained, glad they were crowded so closely together she couldn't see Jake's face.

They left the others at their door, then went on up the stairs, Sarah amused by the look on Grania's face as she watched them go.

'She likes you, Jake.'

'Good. I like her, too. And the others.' He smiled at her. 'One way and another I'm going to enjoy this wedding very much.'

Sarah gave him a narrowed look as he closed the door behind him. 'Why?'

'Because your friends are good company and I'll be spending the day with you.' He waved a hand at the bed. 'Or did you imagine I meant the pleasure of sharing that?'

'No. Though you'll have to,' she said, unruffled. 'There's nowhere else to sleep.'

'So I've noticed. Do you snore?'

Sarah laughed. 'I've no idea. Do you?'

'I've never had complaints,' he said blandly, then gave her the familiar laser-beam look. 'Sarah, I know perfectly well you didn't ask to share because you lust after my body. I'll sleep on the floor. It wouldn't be the first time. So don't let worries about tonight spoil your day.'

Sarah went over to Jake and touched a hand to his cheek. 'You're a lovely man, Jake Hogan.'

To her surprise colour rose in his face as he captured the hand and kissed it. 'Thank you kindly, Miss Tracy. No one's ever said that to me before.'

'You amaze me,' she teased. 'Right, while you hang your things up I'll use the bathroom. Though do take a look inside first.'

Jake crossed the room and stood still on the threshold. 'Good*night*!' He went inside to inspect it, then came out looking smug. 'A bit over-dolphined, but the mirror tiles are Pentiles' best, I'm happy to say. Now put a move on, room-mate, I need a shave.'

Sarah had a very quick shower, then emerged in one of the dressing gowns provided by the management. 'Right. Your turn.'

While Jake was in the bathroom Sarah dressed rapidly, then sat down at the dressing table to do her face, and the hair she'd been up before dawn to wash. She brushed the long, in-curving bob into place, threaded her mother's amethyst and pearl drops through her earlobes, checked the toenails painted the night before in the same clover-pink as her dress, then slid her feet into two strips of kid the colour of her suntanned skin. She got up and did a twirl as Jake came out of the bathroom swathed in the other dressing gown.

'Will I do?'

'Oh, yes, Sarah, you'll do,' he said in a tone which brought swift colour to her face.

'Thank you.' She smiled awkwardly. 'I'll read one of the magazines over there while you get dressed.'

Sarah kept her eyes glued to the pages, well aware that it was idiotic to feel so—so what? Shy? Ridiculous. She'd shared a house for years with Nick and Paul, and with other male students staying from time to time. But none of them had ever been more than friends. Whereas Jake Hogan was something else entirely.

'You can look up,' he said in amusement. 'I'm decent now.'

Sarah cast her magazine aside with relief and watched while Jake fastened a waistcoat in charcoal-grey silk, then knotted a matching tie under his gleaming white collar.

'Will *I* do?' he asked, slotting gold cufflinks into place.

She looked him over in approval, from thick, gold-tipped fair hair, to the gleaming toes of his shoes. Jake appealed to her strongly enough in ordinary clothes, but in formal wedding gear he was spectacular. 'Perfect,' she said. And meant it.

Jake gave her a wry glance. 'If only I were, Sarah.' He checked his watch. 'Time you were putting on your hat.'

Sarah removed the lid from the box, and took out a saucer of white straw decorated with loops of stiff white ribbon and a spray of pink rosebuds in a nest of tulle. 'They added the roses after I took my dress to the shop—good match, aren't they?'

'Perfect. It's a very sexy little hat, but how the devil are you going to anchor it on?' said Jake.

'One of the rosebuds is a hatpin in disguise.' Sarah removed it, planted the hat off centre to let a couple of rosebuds trail over one temple, then speared the confection into place. She turned from the mirror, smiling. 'What do you think?'

He looked at her in silence for a moment. 'I'd better not tell you,' he said at last, and trailed a finger down her cheek, leaving a ribbon of fire on her skin. 'On your mark, get set, then.'

Sarah gathered up a small clutch purse, gave Jake a mocking little curtsy, then made for the door. 'Let's go.'

The wedding ceremony was an informal, riotous affair, with a troupe of small bridesmaids and pageboys who required quelling from time to time while Delphine Bartlett was joined in holy matrimony to Nicholas Morrell. But because the bride turned a beaming smile on the miscreants and obviously didn't mind a bit, no one else did, either. Jake, well versed in the ways of small children, was even able to field a small pageboy making a run for it at one stage, and handed him over with a grin to the perspiring father in pursuit.

'Well done,' whispered Sarah, impressed.

'I'm good with children,' he murmured, and took her hand in his again, to Grania's deep approval.

After the general photo-session later, Tom and Ben took a few shots of their own little group, then Jake took the camera to record the group of friends with the bride and groom and the best man.

'Though why the devil did you have to wear such a gigantic hat, Fran?' grumbled Tom, as he tried to stand close on Jake's instructions.

'It's my sister's Ascot hat,' she retorted. 'It was very good of her to lend it to me.'

'Pity she didn't have a cheeky little number like Sarah's!'

By this time the smaller fry in the wedding party were getting out of hand, and Nick and Delphine made a run for the lych gate, laughing and dodging showers of confetti as they dived into the car for the drive to the bride's home for the wedding breakfast.

'Though why it's breakfast in the afternoon, I'll never know,' said Grania as Ben helped her into the car as if she had *Fragile* marked across her forehead. 'Relax, darling. I'm pregnant, not incapable.'

A marquee, which had served two of the bride's sisters in the past, stood waiting in the sunlit garden of the old rectory, which, according to Nick, the Bartletts had been restoring and renovating ever since their marriage, thirty years before.

'Shall I carry you?' Jake asked as he helped Sarah out into the paddock serving as car park. 'Those shoes aren't made for walking, Miss Tracy.'

'The grass is bone-dry, so I'll manage, thanks.' She smiled at him. 'Come on. This is where you get to kiss the bride.'

'It's not the bride I want to kiss,' he muttered, then grinned as the others joined them, demanding the reason for Sarah's hectic colour.

'It's the heat,' she said, avoiding the gleam in Jake's eye.

After a session of kisses and congratulations the bride and groom circulated amongst the guests, so obviously happy and comfortable together Sarah watched them wistfully until she found Jake's hostile eyes trained on her face.

'Wishing you were the bride?' he asked in an undertone.

'Of course I'm not!' she returned tartly. 'Weddings make women sentimental, that's all.'

He leaned so close his breath was hot on her cheek. 'To me it looked as though you were indulging in a little of the hankering you objected to on my part.'

'What are you two murmuring about?' demanded

Frances. 'Can't have you canoodling at this hour. Have some more champagne.'

'Jake thinks I'm feeling miserable because Nick's married at last,' said Sarah, amused to see she'd startled Jake by her bluntness.

'Why on earth should you be miserable?' asked Grania, surprised.

Ben patted her hand indulgently. 'She means Jake's a bit jealous of Sarah's relationship with Nick, darling.'

'Are you, Jake?' demanded Frances, eyes sparkling.

'Yes,' he said candidly.

'No need,' Grania assured him. 'They were always thick as thieves, of course, but both of them went out with other people all the time. Nick used to moan to Sarah about his love life—though I don't think it was a two-way thing. She was never very communicative about herself.' She smiled. 'She's certainly kept you a dark secret.'

'Would you kindly stop talking about me as though I wasn't here?' complained Sarah, and eyed Jake militantly. 'Happy now?'

'If he's not,' said Tom with a suggestive wink, 'you can always make it up to him later.'

To Sarah's relief the bride and groom chose that moment to join them.

'You look pretty gorgeous, Sal,' said Nick. 'Doesn't she, Jake?'

'Absolutely,' agreed Jake, deadpan, then turned to the bride. 'So do you, Mrs Morrell. I wish you every happiness.'

'Thank you so much.' Delphine exchanged a luminous look with Nick. 'Every time someone calls me Mrs Morrell I get this funny feeling here.' She touched the pearl-embroidered silk at his midriff.

'Me too,' her new husband assured her dotingly.

'You're a very lucky man, Nick,' said Sarah, and gave Delphine a kiss. 'You won't mind if I say I think you're lucky too?'

Later, in the marquee, Tom and Ben switched the place cards so that Sarah sat between them at their table, leaving Jake opposite between their wives.

'Don't be cross; they don't see her very often these days,' said Grania, correctly interpreting the look on Jake's face.

'How could I object with you and Frances for company?' he said, smiling.

When the speeches were over and the cake cut, the top table was cleared away to make room for dancing to records played by a local disc jockey. The bride and groom took to the floor to much affectionate applause, and waltzed slowly and inexpertly round the floor. This time Sarah made sure she displayed no sign of the wistfulness Jake had misunderstood earlier.

When the bridal pair came to a halt the waltz gave way to an old Fred Astaire number, and some of the older guests promptly took to the floor to dance to something familiar while they had the chance.

Jake got up and came round the table to Sarah. 'Dance with me?'

Because her hat had been taken for safe-keeping to the car before the meal, they could have danced cheek to cheek, in tune with the song. But constraint still lingered between them, until at last Sarah raised her head to meet the brooding blue eyes.

'I'm not, you know,' she said, very distinctly.

'Hankering?' He almost tripped her up as he missed a step.

'Yes. At least, not after Nick.' She met his eyes very

deliberately and felt her pulse leap as his lashes dropped to hide his blaze of reaction.

'You mean that?' he muttered into her hair.

Sarah nodded mutely, and moved closer into arms which tightened in response.

From then on the evening was pure bliss for Sarah. She danced once each with Tom and Ben, and even boogied wildly with Nick at one stage, when the music hotted up later in the evening. But for the rest of the time Jake kept her close, either on the dance floor, or sitting with an openly possessive arm round her at the table, to the great satisfaction of Frances and Grania. At last a fanfare blared over the amplifiers and Nick and Delphine reappeared, dressed in travelling clothes.

'Tell us where you're going?' yelled someone.

'Unspecified destination,' said Nick, laughing, then took his bride by the hand and hurried her out to the car, where two sets of parents were waiting to make sure that nothing objectionable was added to the usual assortment of balloons and old boots.

Grania heaved a sentimental sigh as they waved the happy pair off. 'I know the honeymoon's in Mauritius, but I wonder where they're going tonight?'

'Nick said he'd booked the most romantic hotel he could find,' said Sarah.

'He's always told Sarah everything,' said Frances, and patted Jake's hand. 'But don't worry. That's bound to change from now on.'

Jake smiled at her appreciatively, and took Sarah's hand. 'Want to dance some more?'

She glanced at the others—at Grania, drooping against Ben, and Frances, yawning widely. 'Whatever happened to the gang who could party all night?' she teased.

'It's late, it's hellish hot, and we got married!' said Ben. 'Come on, mother of my child. Past your bedtime.'

'Mine too,' yawned Tom.

They said their farewells to the bride's parents, then, due to Grania's current dislike of breakfast, the group arranged to meet in the Greenacres bar at eleven the following morning for coffee before going their separate ways.

'That all went very well,' said Sarah, as she got in the car. 'I can't thank you enough for coming with me, Jake. It made all the difference.'

'No thanks necessary,' he assured her. 'It was a great wedding. Even the speeches were short.'

'Though Nick's was surprisingly sentimental. He's more the flip one-liner type normally.'

'Ah, but he's never been a bridegroom before.'

Back at the hotel they went up in the lift with Ben and Grania, who by this time was speechless with fatigue and heat. When the doors opened on the top floor Ben scooped his wife up in his arms and, with a grinning goodnight to Sarah and Jake, bore his tired, waving little burden off to their room.

'Are you as tired as Grania?' asked Jake, following Sarah up the stairs.

'No. Just terribly hot. But then, I'm not pregnant. At her stage expectant mothers need all the sleep they can get. Even more after the baby arrives,' she added ruefully.

'As you know from experience,' he said, unlocking the door.

In their room lamps were lit and the covers turned down on the bed. Averting her eyes from it, Sarah packed her hat away in its box, then sank down on the settle and with a sigh of relief kicked off the new sandals. 'I may not be as exhausted as Grania, but I'm so hot I couldn't have danced any more tonight.'

'I'm not surprised,' he said, eyeing the tall slender heels. 'How can you even walk in those beats me, let alone dance.'

'It's a girl thing,' she said, laughing.

Jake smiled as she waggled pink-tipped toes. 'You have very pretty feet, Sarah.'

'Really? I'd never thought of feet as pretty, mine or anyone else's.' She looked at them in surprise, then up at Jake. 'It's hot in here. The new bridal suite obviously doesn't run to air-conditioning. Don't you want to get out of that coat?'

'Urgently. But it seemed over-familiar, somehow, to start stripping the moment we came through the door.'

'Go ahead,' she said, curling up as he began to hang his finery away. 'Jake?' she added, once he was down to shirtsleeves.

'Yes, ma'am.' He smiled at her encouragingly.

'We need to talk finances.'

'Why?'

She waved a hand at the room. 'This must be hugely expensive.'

His eyes glittered menacingly. 'Don't even think of offering to share costs.'

'Why not? I would have paid for the other room.'

'But you're not paying for this one.'

Sarah glowered at him. 'Then you can forget about going halves with the wedding present.'

Jake closed the wardrobe door and leaned against it, arms folded, belligerence in every line of him. 'I fail to see why.'

'It's only fair.'

He stared at her in frustration for a moment, then shrugged. 'All right. But I win over the room.'

'OK.' Sarah smiled at him cajolingly. 'Though it makes the next bit awkward, Jake.'

'Go on,' he said, eyes narrowed.

'I'm desperately thirsty. So if I ask to have something sent up will you at least let me pay for drinks?'

'You don't have to.' With a triumphant smile Jake opened the end cupboard door to reveal a small refrigerator and a shelf full of glasses. 'I investigated while you were in the bath earlier on. How about some champagne?'

'I was thinking more of mineral water!'

'There's some of that, too. You can have it later. The champagne's only a half-bottle, so your share won't knock you out. I'll even let you ruin it with fruit juice if you like.'

'How kind!'

Jake half filled a champagne flute and topped it up with orange juice, poured a glass of wine for himself, then opened the windows to the sultry night before he sat down on the chair drawn up to Sarah's settle. 'I think we've toasted the bride and groom well and truly already, so this one's for us,' he said, touching his glass to hers.

'To us,' repeated Sarah, and sipped her drink. 'Mmm, lovely. In fact the entire day was lovely, Jake. Except for one particular incident,' she added tartly.

He shrugged. 'Sorry about that. You were looking at Nick with such yearning in your eyes I was jealous as hell.'

'It was envy, not yearning, Jake.' She drained her glass and put it down on the table. 'Nick's the last of my crowd to get married, which leaves me as the only single one left. For a moment I couldn't help envying the security the others take for granted in their relationships.'

Jake nodded slowly. 'Whereas you bring Davy up alone.'

Sarah reached out to touch his hand. 'Which is no hardship, Jake, I assure you. Blame my split-second of envy on wedding-day emotion. I was back on course right away, I promise.'

'Good. By the way, talking of Davy, she told me that Polly's dad is running in the fathers' race on sports day,' said Jake, the sudden change of subject startling Sarah considerably.

'She didn't tell me there was a fathers' race—oh, *no*!' She eyed him in alarm. 'I suppose that means there's a mothers' race, too.'

'Oh, yes. And Davy's entered you for it.' Jake's lips twitched. 'That's not all. At the Rogers' lunch she suggested I run in the fathers' race with Don, but I had to explain that, not being a father, I wasn't eligible.'

'Good heavens!' said Sarah, astounded. 'She never said a word to me, the monkey. Sorry she put you on the spot like that.'

'*I'm* not sorry. I took it as a good sign.'

'Of what?'

'That she approves of me, possibly even likes me. Which,' added Jake, putting his glass down, 'brings me to a subject I've been waiting for the right time to discuss.'

'What is it?' she said warily.

His eyes locked on Sarah's. 'When I booked this room I didn't foresee that you'd be sharing it with me. But now you're a captive audience I have something to say. So listen, Sarah.'

'For heaven's sake, Jake,' she said impatiently, 'you're making me nervous. Just say it, whatever it is.'

He stood up abruptly, something in his attitude sending Sarah's heart racing with apprehension by the time he spoke.

'You must know that I'm in love with you,' he said at last, taking her breath away. 'And I believe you're not indifferent to me, either. Is that true?'

Sarah nodded mutely, her eyes fixed on his.

'I've thought about this a lot,' he went on. 'And it's obvious you won't allow yourself anything warmer than friendship with me, or even let yourself respond to me normally, because of what happened first time round.'

'But—'

He held up a hand. 'Let me finish. With you I want— need—so much more than friendship.' Jake breathed in deeply, a pulse throbbing beside his mouth. 'I know I said brave things about being satisfied with whatever relationship you wanted. But the kind *I* want, darling, is marriage.'

CHAPTER NINE

BECAUSE her heart was pounding and the room was very warm, Sarah sat perfectly still, needing all her energy just to breathe. 'You say you've given this thought,' she said at last.

Jake sat down again, long legs outstretched, the animation draining from his face. 'Do I take that as a no?'

She gave him a long, troubled look. 'Have you taken Davy into consideration?'

'Of course I have.'

'But you're only thirty years old, Jake. Which is pretty young to take on a nine-year-old child.'

'Older than you,' he pointed out.

'That's different.'

'I know. You're her mother. But, unlike your defecting friend, I'm sure I could make a good stepfather. I like Davy. And maybe I don't shape up to Don Rogers in her eyes, but I think she likes me. Or could do, given the chance to get to know me.' He turned to look at her. 'You won't expose Davy to any temporary arrangement with a man in case she gets hurt. I understand that. But in this case temporary doesn't come into it. I want you for keeps, Sarah. Both of you.'

Sarah blinked, then blinked again more rapidly, but tears poured down her cheeks, and, lacking something to mop them up, she knuckled them from her eyes and gave a loud, unromantic sniff.

Jake got up to fetch a container of tissues from the

bathroom. 'Compliments of the management,' he said, handing it to her.

Sarah mopped her eyes, blew her nose, then gave him a damp smile of apology. 'Sorry about that. I don't do tears much.'

Jake swung her feet to the floor and sat down, putting his arm round her shoulders. 'I didn't mean to make you cry. And if the thought of marrying me affects you like that perhaps we'd better forget all about it.'

Easier said than done, thought Sarah despairingly. Until he'd brought the subject up she'd had no idea she wanted to marry Jake. Or hadn't allowed herself to consider the possibility.

'If we did marry,' she began, tensing as she felt his arm tighten, 'wouldn't your family find it strange you'd chosen a woman with a child, rather than a more conventional bride?'

'I've no idea,' he said, shrugging. 'If you were past the age of having more children it would be different. But you're what? Twenty-seven?'

She nodded.

He raised her face to his, giving the smile that did such damage to her defences. 'I'm sure we could provide Davy with a couple of siblings with no trouble at all, my darling.'

It wasn't fair, she thought in anguish. The endearment, reinforced by a clamouring voice in her head which urged her to say yes, was hard to fight. Suddenly her resistance vanished, and she yielded to the arms which closed round her. Why should she fight? It would be so good to have a man in her life. And not just any man, but one she could trust, and who was happy to include Davy in his proposal.

'Jake,' she said at last, raising her head. 'I know this

isn't the answer you deserve, but would you give me a little time to think it over?'

He gave her a searching look, then shook his head. 'I'd like to be noble and say take as much time as you want. But if you're going to turn me down I'd rather you did it now—made it a clean break.'

Sarah felt a rush of pure dismay. 'So if I say no that's it? Over and out?'

'I want you for my wife, Sarah, with everything the word implies. I won't settle for anything less.' His eyes darkened. 'Do you feel anything for me at all?'

'You know very well that I do,' she said with heat, and detached herself from his hold. 'In fact, I can't think straight when I'm so close to you.'

'Which is encouraging,' he said wryly as she stood up.

'Jake,' said Sarah with sudden decision. 'If you'll wait until morning I'll give you my answer then.'

'A recipe for a sleepless night, if ever I heard one! Not,' added Jake, heaving a sigh, 'that it was going to be restful anyway.' He got up and gave her a swift, hard kiss. 'Go on. You take the bathroom first. In the meantime I shall pitch my tent.'

Sarah gave him a grateful smile. 'Thank you, Jake.'

'What for this time?'

'For the proposal. It's my first.'

He narrowed his eyes at her. 'And last, too, if I have anything to do with it.'

When Sarah came out of the bathroom, feeling desperately hot in the hotel dressing gown over her cotton nightshirt, Jake had set up a makeshift bed on the floor, with blankets and a pillow.

'That looks horribly uncomfortable,' she said, eyeing

it guiltily. 'This is all my fault. I shouldn't have asked to share.'

'I could hardly make the suggestion myself,' he pointed out. 'But the moment I heard Grania was expecting a baby I began trying to work out some way of giving her my room without embarrassing you.'

She grinned. 'It would have been pretty hard for Grania and Frances to swallow that we weren't sleeping together.'

'Why?'

'Because they think you're a charmer, and sexy with it!'

'I only wish you shared their enthusiasm,' he said dryly.

Sarah gave him a wry little smile. 'Actually, I do.'

With a growl Jake started towards her, stopped dead, then turned on his heel and strode off to the bathroom, slamming the door shut behind him.

Sarah took off the dressing gown and slid under the covers, then turned off the lamp at her side of the bed. This, she thought despondently, was going to be a long, long night. She felt hot and restless, but forced herself to keep very still when Jake crossed the room to turn off the other lamp. She waited, perspiration beading her upper lip. And knew she had no earthly right to feel disappointed when he let himself down on the floor instead of sliding into bed with her.

Convinced that heat and tension would keep her awake all night, Sarah lay so still that eventually she dozed, only to wake with a violent start as the room lit up and thunder rolled. The curtains blew out into the room on a gush of hot wind as rain sheeted down outside, and she lay rigid, heart hammering, determined not to make a sound. But when the storm moved ominously closer she burrowed under the pillows to shut out the lightning which lit up the room. They were insulation neither against the noise, nor against her gasp of fright. Jake got up to close the windows against the rain blowing in, then switched on the lamp. He sat on the edge of the bed, removed the pillows and pulled Sarah into his arms.

'Are you all right?' he asked, smoothing her hair as she hid her face against his bare chest.

'No, I'm not!' she wailed as another crack of thunder shook the room.

'Don't worry. There's a lightning conductor on the roof,' he said into her ear. 'You're shivering. Are you cold?'

She shook her head vehemently. 'Anything but. Sorry about this, Jake. I'd better shut myself in the bathroom until it's over.'

'There's a window in there, too,' he pointed out. 'Festooned with dolphins, but not lightning-proof.'

Sarah gave a smothered scream as lightning forked through the room a split-second before thunder cracked overhead. She clung on to Jake for dear life, and he went rigid for a moment, then laid her back down on the bed.

Sarah gazed up at him beseechingly. 'Don't leave me!'

Jake looked down at her, jaw clenched, then he slid in beside her, drew her into his arms, tucked her head against his shoulder and pulled the sheet over them both. 'Is that better?'

'Better' didn't begin to describe it, thought Sarah as another crack of thunder propelled her against him. 'Much better,' she whispered against his throat.

Jake lay motionless as an effigy, but Sarah felt heat baking from his body into hers, and her heart thumped when she registered that his only covering was a pair of thin cotton boxers. Which were no disguise for his arousal.

When another crack of thunder sent her burrowing closer Jake groaned and tried to thrust her away, but Sarah clung to him with such desperation his control abruptly snapped. His arms closed round her like steel bands, making it impossible for her to flinch away. He kissed her hungrily, savagely, his mouth ravaging hers as though the elements had stripped away the charm to leave the basic man in command. His lips and tongue demanded a response she gave with such abandon the breath tore through his chest as his pillaging mouth left hers to move down her throat. His hands slid up her thighs to caress the outline of her hips and waist, then he stripped the nightshirt over her head and tossed it on the floor. Lying propped on an elbow, Jake hung over her, his fingers tracing a path from her parted mouth to her thighs, the silence broken only by their rapid breathing now the storm had begun to move away. Sarah knew that he was giving her the opportunity to change her mind, to draw back as she always had long before this stage was reached. But for the first time it was different. She wanted this. She wanted Jake. When she held up her arms in fierce entreaty his eyes lit with such heat her breath caught as his hands slid upwards to cup her breasts and lift them to his hungry mouth.

'Jake, I must—' she gasped, but he swung his body over hers and stifled her words with a kiss so explicit it sent everything out of her head.

'Don't stop me now, darling,' he breathed against her lips. 'I want you so much it hurts. But I want you to need this as much as I do.'

He went on kissing her, and she gave a stifled moan

as his mouth moved down to join the fingers caressing her breasts. Sarah shivered at the almost unbearable feelings he was plucking from deep inside her as he pulled on each sensitised nipple, igniting all the need he could ever want. Jake slid a hand between her thighs to find the hot, liquid proof of it, and drew in a deep, unsteady breath of pure satisfaction, his eyes holding hers as his long, expert fingers caused waves of sensation which flooded her with such hot, throbbing pleasure she choked back a scream, then lay with astonished eyes still locked with his as the aftershocks faded. He smiled triumphantly and kissed her parted mouth, then slid over her to lie between her thighs.

'Jake—' she tried again, but he laid a finger on her lips.

'Do you want me?' he demanded.

'*Yes*. Desperately—but I've never done this before!' she blurted.

Jake stared at her in utter disbelief. He would have pulled away, but Sarah revolved her hips against his in fierce demand. 'This is how much I want you,' she said through her teeth. 'So, having got this far, you'd better make love to me now or I'll go mad. *Please!*'

Jake needed no second bidding. He entered her with a smooth thrust she responded to with a sharp intake of breath at the small, tearing pain of it. His head flew up, but Sarah smiled up into his questioning eyes and locked her hands behind his neck. 'Don't stop!'

'I can't,' he groaned, and moved inside her. Sarah made a relishing little sound of appreciation, discovering that pain had been replaced by pleasure which grew fiercer and hotter as Jake made love to her with all the skill at his command. Her emotions heightened by the storm, Sarah responded with such fervour to the unfamiliar bliss of possession that his careful expertise quickly deserted him, and he crushed her close as they surged together towards fulfilment which overtook him long before he'd intended, and he lay gasping in her arms in the throes of a climax he knew she hadn't shared.

'Darling, I'm *sorry*,' he groaned, and rubbed his cheek against hers in contrition.

Sarah gave him a lazy, exultant smile. 'Don't be. One each. Only fair.'

Jake laughed deep in his throat, and smoothed the damp hair away from her forehead. 'Next time,' he promised, 'we'll make it together.'

He rolled over onto his back and drew her against him, one hand smoothing her hair as their heartbeats slowed. Sarah felt such a wave of love for him she heaved in a deep, tremulous sigh and reached up to kiss him.

'Thank you,' he whispered. 'Was that for anything in particular?'

'Your extraordinary forbearance.'

Jake turned his head to look at her, making no attempt to misunderstand. 'I love you, Sarah. And I admit I'm poleaxed. Neither of which entitles me to ask questions you're not ready to answer.'

'Yes, it does,' she said at once, and smiled at him. 'If we are going to marry—'

'No doubt about it,' he assured her with arrogance.

'Then you deserve an explanation.'

Jake looked at her in silence for a moment. His eyes, reverted now to their normal colour, were thoughtful. 'I won't deny that part of me is burning with curiosity, my darling. But before any explanations let's have a drink and just relax for a while.'

Sarah agreed gratefully. Her emotions were running so high it seemed a good idea to calm down for a while before she told him the truth about Davy. 'Only I'll have that mineral water this time.'

Jake pulled the sheet over her, then went to the drinks cupboard and filled two glasses with a mixture of mineral water and fruit juice.

'Nothing stronger for you?' Sarah said, surprised.

Jake sat beside her and leaned against the pillows, smiling into her eyes. 'No. I'm intoxicated enough already.'

She gave him a speaking look of thanks, drained the glass quickly, set it down on the bedside table, then wriggled close to him. 'It's been a very eventful day.'

Jake finished his own drink, then put his arms round her. 'And night,' he added, rubbing his cheek over her hair. 'And just in case you have any doubts I'm spending the rest of it right here in this bed. With you.'

'Of course you are.' She smiled up at him. 'Because you don't snore, Jake. At least you haven't done so far.'

He grinned. 'Probably because I haven't been to sleep.'

'No wonder. It must have been horribly uncomfortable on the floor,' she said with sympathy.

'That was only a contributory factor. The real reason for my insomnia was right here, in this bed but out of reach.' Jake kissed her. 'How did you expect me to sleep in those circumstances?'

'I'm not out of reach now,' she pointed out.

'No,' he agreed huskily, and pulled her closer. 'Are you tired, darling?'

'Not in the least,' she said, surprised to find she was right. 'I thought people went straight to sleep after making love.'

'We obviously haven't made love enough yet,' he said promptly, and Sarah laughed.

'If you're going to make love to me again, Jake—'

'No if about it!'

'Then I'd like a shower first.'

'Brilliant idea.' He slid out of bed and held out his hand.

In spite of sharing the ultimate intimacy with Jake only minutes before, Sarah felt irrationally shy as she slid naked from the bed. Colour flooded her face when her nipples hardened in response to his caressing gaze. His breathing suddenly rapid, Jake picked her up and carried her into the bathroom to set her on her feet in the shower stall. He turned on the spray and held her close against him, kissing her as he smoothed scented gel over her hot, wet body, and Sarah did the same for him in return, no longer shy at all. He groaned like a man in pain as her seeking hands brought him to full arousal, and he switched off the spray and parted her thighs with an invading knee. They clung together in hot, wet contact as they kissed with increasing wildness, until at last Jake tore his mouth away, snatched up a towel to dry her with unsteady, urgent hands, then carried her back to bed.

They surged together at once, all preliminaries swept aside. Mouth to mouth, hands entwined, their bodies fused together in a union Jake fought to keep slow and gradual. But soon Sarah was overwhelmed by the pulsing reality of her first climax, and, feeling her innermost muscles clenched round him, Jake released his control and collapsed on her, gasping endearments against her parted mouth.

It was a long time before either of them had the breath

or inclination to speak. At last Jake turned over on his back and pulled Sarah close.

'This,' he said gruffly, 'is where one asks how was it for you?'

She smiled up at him, her gold-flecked eyes glittering in the lamplight. 'Does one?'

'I thought you might be unfamiliar with the protocol. In the circumstances,' he added, pulling her higher so he could kiss her.

'Because I'm new at it, you mean.'

'Precisely. An extraordinary, glorious fact I'm still trying to take in.' He let out a deep, unsteady breath. 'I'm very grateful to the storm for making you seduce me.'

Sarah reared up in indignation. 'Is that what I did?'

'In a way.' Jake smoothed her tumbled hair, his eyes suddenly sober. 'I wouldn't have initiated this myself, darling. Not tonight, anyway.'

'Why not?'

'Because I was damned if I'd take advantage of the situation.'

'Halo problems again,' she chuckled, and rubbed her cheek against his bare shoulder. 'You're one of a kind, Jake Hogan.'

He glowered at her. 'I'm not, you know.'

'All right, all right. I won't talk about halos again.'

'Good. Because human failings are beginning to get the better of me right now.'

'Curiosity?'

'Absolutely.' Jake sat up, rearranged the pillows and held out his arms.

Sarah slid into them with a sigh of pleasure as he drew the sheet over them. 'At least you can now understand why I wouldn't—couldn't let myself respond to you,

Jake.' She looked up at him with sombre eyes. 'In college it was no problem to duck out of all the bed-hopping the others were involved in. Nor with anyone since. But with you, for the first time, I wanted this almost from the start. Even though it meant letting you into the secret I've never shared with anyone.'

'I still can't take it in,' Jake said, equally grave, and kissed her gently. 'Davy's so like you I just can't believe she's not your child.'

Sarah's eyes filled with unshed tears. 'She is mine in every way that matters, Jake, just not my actual daughter. Davina Anne Tracy is my sister.'

CHAPTER TEN

'YOUR *sister*?' Jake stared at Sarah incredulously, then slid out of bed, shrugged on the robe and fetched the tissues, holding her in his arms while he blotted her eyes with such tender care the tears overflowed.

'Sorry, sorry.' She rubbed her wet face against his chest. 'Tears twice in one night. Personal best for S. Tracy.'

Jake waited until she was calmer, then fetched a shot glass from the minibar. 'Medicinal cognac. Down with it, darling.'

Sarah drank the mouthful of fiery spirit, and felt better as the warmth spread through her. She coughed a little as she handed Jake the glass. 'Thank you. Though I hate the stuff—I hate to think of your hotel bill in the morning, too.'

He said something rude about the bill, then got back into bed beside her. 'Sarah,' he said firmly, as she curled up against him, 'if it makes you unhappy, don't tell me any more.'

She touched a hand to his cheek in gratitude, but shook her head. 'I want you to know everything, Jake. And I won't cry again. Promise.'

The story began one bleak January day with a funeral. David Tracy had just gone back from leave to the work he was doing on a hotel construction in Malaysia, and because Sarah had been back in school after the Christmas holidays, and working hard for exams, Anne had left her in Campden Road with her grandmother and made the long journey to Cumbria alone.

'When she was doing her teacher training,' Sarah told Jake, 'my mother had a friend called Tony Barrett. They were very close, rather like Nick and me. Best of friends. They went to each other's weddings, and the two couples got on well together. For years Tony brought his wife Lisa to visit us, and we went up to Cumbria to visit them.'

Anne Tracy had gone to see Lisa Barrett twice during her long, protracted illness, and the moment Tony rang to say his wife had finally died Anne had set off for Cumbria again. After the funeral, when all the guests and relatives had gone, Tony had begged Anne to stay on for a day or so to help him sort through his wife's belongings. The first night alone in the house together, when he'd gone to her room in desperate distress, her only thought had been to comfort him.

'My mother was small, and Tony Barrett was a big man,' said Sarah without inflection. 'And due to his wife's illness he'd been celibate for a very long time.'

'So the inevitable happened,' said Jake quietly.

Tony Barrett had been wild with remorse afterwards, and Anne Tracy, sick with misery and guilt over the entire episode, had driven home at first light, determined to block it out and never think of it again.

'I was shaping up for A-levels, and too taken up with my own concerns for a while to notice that my mother was quieter than usual after she came back,' Sarah said remorsefully.

But eventually Sarah had noticed, and grown worried. Anne had looked haggard from loss of sleep, and tried so hard to be bright and animated Sarah had known that underneath something was terribly wrong.

'So I demanded to know if she had cancer, like Lisa Barrett.' Sarah heaved a sigh. 'It shocked her into telling me she was pregnant. At first I was so relieved to know she wasn't terminally ill I couldn't understand why she was in such a state about being pregnant. She was only thirty-nine. Finally she broke down, and told me that not only was Tony Barrett to blame, but that she'd had such a bad time when I was born that my father insisted on a vasectomy. It was the thought of telling him which was killing her.'

'God,' said Jake, wincing. 'What a situation.'

Margaret Parker had been appalled when Anne finally confessed the truth, and in her frantic desire to avoid scandal had instantly advised abortion. But Anne, who'd had strong beliefs on the subject, hadn't been able to bear the thought of that. But she hadn't been able to bear the thought of causing her husband so much hurt, either, and had become so distraught that the entire subject had had to be dropped for a while.

'Grandma insisted on moving in with us during that awful time,' said Sarah. 'She told me she was afraid to leave Mother alone while I was in school, but, looking back, I'm sure she used the time to keep hammering at her to get rid of the baby.'

'Your father wasn't told?' asked Jake.

'No. In spite of my grandmother's attitude, Mother was looking and feeling much better by the time he came home on leave. Grandma went back to Campden Road, and my parents were so happy just to be together again Mother couldn't bear to spoil things for Dad. Before he went back to Malaysia he told her he intended to see the job out before he came home again, which meant autumn at the earliest. Normally Mother would have been in despair at the long parting, but for once she was relieved.'

'Did she see a doctor?' asked Jake.

Sarah shook her head. 'We lived in a small village where everyone knew everyone else. My father was born and brought up there, and the doctor was his personal friend.'

Jake was silent for a moment, frowning. 'All this was a heavy load for a teenager to cope with, Sarah.'

'Even heavier for my mother, Jake.'

The unwanted baby had been due to arrive some time in early autumn, and the moment Sarah finished her exams that June Margaret Parker had insisted the three of them went off to Cornwall for the rest of the summer.

'We did that every year anyway,' said Sarah. 'Polruan Cottage stood on its own, a fair way out of the nearest village, and although even by that stage Mother didn't look pregnant, she refused to go a step farther than the garden. I'm convinced she'd persuaded herself that because she didn't want the baby she'd miscarry and Dad would never have to know.'

'But surely she was in need of medical attention?'

Sarah nodded. 'That was part of Grandma's reason for moving us down there once abortion was no longer a possibility. It was her home turf, and her oldest friend had once been a midwife. Mrs Treharne was let in on the secret, sworn to silence, and checked on Mother regularly. Life got easier after that.'

The advent of Jenna Treharne had been very necessary one evening in July, when, right in the middle of a violent thunderstorm, it had seemed that Anne's wish was about to be granted and she'd gone into premature labour. Deaf to her patient's protests, Jenna had called am ambulance and accompanied Anne and Margaret in it to the hospital in Truro, leaving Sarah, who had not long passed her driving test, to follow them alone in her grandmother's car, not only rigid with terror when lightning forked around her as she drove through the rain, but desperately afraid her mother would be dead before she got to the hospital. But it had been hours later when Anne Tracy, exhausted and in need of a blood transfusion, gave birth to her daughter. And though baby Davina had been a couple of pounds lighter than she would have weighed full-term, she'd been in remarkably good shape otherwise.

'Mother was kept in hospital while Davy had a stay in an incubator before they were discharged,' said Sarah. 'And after they got back to Polruan Cottage the baby was fine. Mother was the problem.'

Because her closest friends knew about the vasectomy Anne had been in despair about returning to her own home with a baby. She'd been in a poor state physically after the birth, and mentally at such a low ebb that Jenna had given dire warnings of clinical depression, and worse. So Margaret had taken complete charge of Anne while Sarah looked after the baby right from the first, taking the hard work involved in her stride. Because she'd been young and fit Sarah had soon got used to broken nights, and nappy changes, and the endless round of sterilising and making up bottle feeds. It had been the arguments with her grandmother which were hardest to bear, because Margaret Parker had kept urging Anne to have the baby adopted.

'By that time,' said Sarah, 'I felt that Davina belonged to me. My baby. I couldn't bear the idea of adoption. Nor could my mother. Then my grandmother said something that made it all so simple.'

'What was that, sweetheart?' asked Jake, holding her closer.

'In one of her outbursts she said it would have been far better if the baby had been mine. There would have been tongue-wagging, but because I was so young it would have been accepted more easily—by my father as well as everyone else.' Sarah breathed in deeply. 'Afterwards, when my mother was asleep, Grandma persuaded me to claim Davy as mine. Somehow she'd got it into her head that I was to blame for everything. That if I had gone to Cumbria with Mother, instead of insisting on staying home to study, none of it would have happened.'

'How on earth did she work that one out?' said Jake, incensed.

'She wasn't very rational at the time. But once I'd thought it over I decided for myself that it was the best thing to do. Not,' added Sarah fiercely, 'for my grandmother's sake, but for my mother and father and their marriage. So next day I went to register Davy's birth, and the registrar took it for granted I was the mother anyway. Which means the birth certificate reads: "Mother—Sarah Anne Tracy. Father—blank."'

'What a crazily brave thing to do.' Jake looked down at her in wonder. 'You do know that giving false information like that is illegal?'

'My mother's name was Sarah Anne, like me. She called herself Anne. So it seemed almost right...'

Jake shook his head. 'And no one ever questioned it?'

'My mother went up like a rocket. For a while I was terrified I'd sent her over the edge. But after endless arguments I hit below the belt and pointed out the grief it would save my father. And because of my grandmother's desperate urging Mother, who was in no fit state to put up a fight, finally capitulated. Though not without a long list of conditions, mainly about my education. As for my reception back home—' Sarah shrugged. 'I'd had a struggle with my weight as a teenager. So when I returned from Cornwall with a baby, weighing a stone less due to stress and sheer hard work, it caused the expected stir, but no one ever doubted that Davy was mine.'

Jake rubbed his cheek over her hair. 'But you'd been born and brought up in your village, too, darling. Didn't you mind?'

'Of course I did. But I didn't have a boyfriend, so I knew no blame could be attached to anyone. And I'd already left school. But I admit it hurt badly when my so-called best friend took off in a huff because I refused to tell her about Davy's father.' Sarah shrugged. 'But none of that was important against saving my parents' marriage. I cancelled my gap year *au pair* job in France, and because my mother was still so fragile I looked after Davy myself. So from the day she was born she was all mine.'

The worst part for Sarah, once Davy had safely arrived, had been writing to her father to give him news which, however well-intentioned, was nevertheless a lie. But David Tracy had rung the moment he had her letter, accepted Sarah's refusal to name the father, and assured his daughter of his love and support, and his willingness to help Anne with the baby as long as Sarah agreed to take up her college place, as planned. By the time he'd eventually come home for good Anne had fully recovered physically, and was so happy to be reunited with her husband that, all too aware of the alternative, she'd finally achieved total acceptance of Sarah's quixotic gesture.

'And, seeing them so happy together, I never regretted it for a minute,' said Sarah. 'For that first year I insisted on looking after Davy full-time, but Mother took over when I went to university, and with Dad's help looked after her baby herself—as she'd wanted to all along. It was a terrible wrench for me to leave Davy, but I was normal teenager enough to enjoy the usual student scene once I was part of it. Though I went home a lot more often than the friends I made because I couldn't bear to be parted long from Davy.' She smiled up at Jake. 'She adored my parents, but *I* was Mummy.'

Sarah had eventually achieved her English degree, and returned to live at home while she followed it up with a computer course. Eventually she'd got a job in a software firm, and shared Davy with her parents.

'Then when she was five they went on holiday and never came back. They were killed when the coach transferring them from hotel to airport crashed. And my life changed completely. Left with full responsibility for Davy, I had to sell the family home, which had been mortgaged to put me through college and pay Davy's school fees, so it didn't fetch as much as expected. It just gave me a bit of a cushion in the bank, so I could take a part-time job, but we had to move in with my grandmother. Which wasn't an ideal situation for either of us, but it won her no end of brownie points with her friends. The rest you know.' Sarah gave a sudden, inelegant yawn. 'Sorry, Jake! Confession may be good for the soul, but it's jolly tiring.'

'It's been a long, eventful day,' said Jake, settling her close against him. 'It's an amazing story, Sarah. But just one more thing. Was this Tony Barrett ever told about Davy?'

Sarah shook her head. 'No. It was one of the conditions Mother made when I wouldn't let her tell Dad the truth. But because she refused to have anything to do with him afterwards I always felt sorry for him, so maybe one day, when Davy's old enough to cope with the truth herself, I'll leave it to her to decide whether she wants to get in touch with Tony.' She smiled ruefully. 'He doesn't have any children, so there's no gothic-novel possibility of Davy falling in love with her brother one day.'

When Sarah woke the sky was just getting light, and she was still held fast in Jake's arms. She moved a little, his lashes flew up and his eyes, vividly blue in the morning light, lit up as they met hers.

'Good morning,' she whispered.

'A fantastic morning,' he agreed, kissing her nose. 'Did you sleep well?'

'I must have done. I've only just surfaced. So you obviously don't snore.'

'Of course I don't. You don't, either.'

'That's a relief.' She stretched luxuriously, and felt him tense against her.

'If you do that,' he warned in a constricted tone, 'there could be consequences.'

Sarah looked up into the darkening blue eyes, and smiled into them as she deliberately stretched again.

Jake gave a stifled laugh and held her closer. 'Tell me, Miss Tracy, what are your views on making love by dawn's early light?'

'I don't have any, Mr Hogan—yet,' she said provocatively.

'Something I'd better put right, then. Another first,' he added with blatantly male satisfaction, and began to pay slow, subtle attention to every inch of her until Sarah made it passionately clear she could endure the delicious agony no longer, and Jake surged inside her to take her on a fiery, gasping quest for the rapture they achieved almost in unison.

It was a long time before either of them spoke afterwards, but at last Jake raised his head. 'Well?' he demanded.

Sarah let out a deep, unsteady breath. 'I now realise why the others were so keen on this.'

'The others?'

'The other students I knew. Those you've met, and a lot more besides. I was the only one who kept my bed strictly to myself.'

Jake propped himself up on an elbow to look down into her face. 'You must have had a few problems with that?'

'Quite a lot, at first. But eventually it was taken for granted that my experience with Davy was the problem.' Sarah smiled up at him. 'You're the only one who knows the truth.'

Jake trailed a caressing finger down her cheek. 'I still can't believe I was your first lover. I thought I was dreaming when—'

'When I ordered you to make love to me?'

'Orders I was deliriously happy to obey!' Jake kissed her at length, then rubbed his cheek against hers. 'Tell me you love me.'

Her dark eyes narrowed ominously. 'If I didn't, Jake Hogan, none of this would have happened in the first place. Storm or no storm.'

'Tell me just the same,' he commanded.

To Sarah's embarrassment shyness overtook her again. 'I love you,' she muttered, eyes falling.

'Again.'

She stared up at him resentfully. 'If you keep on making me say it I might change my mind.'

'In which case,' said Jake very softly, 'I'd have to resort to measures to change it back.'

The mere thought of the measures he had in mind hurried Sarah's breathing. Then her stomach gave a loud, embarrassing grumble, and he threw back his head and laughed.

'You're hungry!' Jake bent his tousled head to kiss the place which protested. His lips lingered, moved downward, then stopped abruptly.

'What's the matter?' she demanded.

He raised his head to give her a smile which made her toes curl. 'Making love to you, Sarah Tracy, is addictive.'

Sarah flushed and looked away. 'If you'll hand me the dressing gown I'll have a bath. What time's breakfast?'

'Eight o'clock, right here. I ordered it last night. Though we can eat downstairs if you prefer.'

'I don't. I'd much rather have it here, in private. But I hope you ordered a lot of food!' She smiled at him as she scrambled into her robe. 'Shan't be long. I'm off to play with the dolphins.'

He sighed. 'Alone, I suppose.'

'If breakfast is arriving at eight,' she retorted, 'very definitely alone!'

After the emotional and physical demands of the night Sarah felt tired, but utterly happy as she shared breakfast with Jake.

'I wasn't sure what you'd like,' he told her, 'so I took a chance. Coffee, fresh fruit compote, scrambled eggs with grilled bacon, plus the usual toast and butter and so on.'

'Perfect.' Sarah tucked in with gusto. 'I never eat much breakfast normally, but I'm hungry this morning.'

'So am I.' He leaned close to kiss her cheek. 'Our recent activities tend to do that.'

'Do they?' Sarah gave him a sparkling, gold-flecked glance. 'You'd know more about that than me.'

'True.' Jake was abruptly serious. 'But this is a first for me, too, Sarah. I don't deny that there have been women in my life before. Women whose company I enjoyed. But with you it's different.'

'Why?'

'Because I've never loved anyone before,' he said simply.

She gave him a luminous, rather shaky smile. 'Thank you, darling.'

'Say that again.'

'Thank you?'

He leaned nearer. 'No. The darling bit.'

She brandished her fork at him. 'I want to get on with my breakfast, my darling Mr Hogan, so let's leave the endearments until later.'

Later, packed and ready to join the others for coffee, Sarah sighed regretfully as she took a last look around the room.

'Are you glad I persuaded them to let me have the bridal suite?' said Jake.

Sarah nodded fervently. 'Because we were the first to sleep here it seems like ours. I hate to leave it.'

'We can come back any time you like.' Jake looked down at her with the familiar straight look. 'Which brings me to the next important subject. How soon can we get married?'

'If it were just up to me I'd say as soon as possible,'

she assured him. 'But there's Davy to consider. I'd like to give her time to get used to the idea.'

'Do *you* need time?'

She gave him a wicked little smile. 'None at all. You've sold me on the idea already.'

When they went downstairs to the bar the others were waiting for them.

'Good morning, you two,' said Frances, smiling. 'We thought of you last night, Sarah. I hope you cuddled her during the storm, Jake.'

He grinned. 'I rather enjoyed the storm myself.'

'I bet you did,' said Ben with relish, as the others laughed.

'We're embarrassing Sarah,' said Grania quickly.

'Not in the least,' said Sarah, and exchanged a long look with Jake. 'In fact we've got something to tell you.'

Jake kissed her swiftly, then turned to the others with a triumphant smile. 'Last night I asked Sarah to marry me. And she said yes.'

After their announcement, it was a long time before Sarah and Jake managed to make their farewells, and head for home.

'It occurred to me, too late, that maybe you might not want our intentions made quite so public yet—if at all,' said Sarah, when they were finally on their way.

'Are you serious? I want the whole world to know—a.s.a.p. But Davy first, obviously. So how do we approach that?'

Sarah gave it some thought. 'Perhaps you'd like to take us both to the Trout on Saturday evening, to eat in the garden there if it's fine. Davy would love going out for a grown-up dinner.'

'Done,' he said promptly. 'Will you tell her straight away?'

'No. I'll wait until Sunday morning, after she's spent time with you.' She smiled at him. 'So you'd better put on the charm for Saturday night.'

To her surprise Jake was unamused.

'I never deliberately set out to charm, Sarah,' he said shortly. 'And even if I did I would never try it with Davy.'

Sarah touched his hand in penitence. 'I'm sorry. You obviously didn't like that. But I witnessed your masterly performance with the receptionist, remember?'

He nodded, keeping his eyes on the road. 'I admit that I pull out the stops when absolutely necessary. But never with you, Sarah. You get the plain, unvarnished Jake Hogan, always.'

'Which is all I want, ever,' she assured him.

They stopped for a snack after they left the motorway, then drove back in the afternoon to Campden Road.

'Gosh, I'm tired,' said Sarah, as they went inside the quiet house. She smiled at him. 'You must be, too.'

'We had very little sleep last night,' he reminded her, taking her into his arms. 'I suggest you go to bed for a while, darling. On your own, unfortunately. I'm just going to check on things at Pentiles, then I'll take my gear on to the flat. What time shall I come back?'

'Whenever you like. I'll make supper.'

'Perfect.' He kissed her swiftly. 'Then after that let's have an early night. Together.'

'Even more perfect,' she assured him, and kissed him back at such length Jake lost all enthusiasm for anything to do with work.

'Go,' said Sarah, pushing him away. 'I'll be waiting when you come back. About eight?'

Jake shook his head as he went to the door. 'Seven.'

Instead of taking a nap Sarah rang the school to report that she was back home in Campden Road. Then, feeling that the occasion called for something special by way of a meal, she got the car out to go shopping for food. She rushed home with her spoils afterwards, had a bath instead of a rest, then set to with a will in the kitchen. A few minutes short of seven she was dressed and ready in a sleeveless white T-shirt dress, her hair shining and her face alight with a glow which owed nothing to cosmetics. The courgette flowers she'd splurged on were stuffed with a savoury cheese mixture, ready to deep fry, a salad lacked only its dressing, and two steaks waited in a marinade, ready to grill. She'd laid the kitchen table with a yellow cloth, and as a finishing touch put out blue saucers to hold the fat yellow candles she'd bought.

When the phone rang Sarah went cold. Jake wasn't coming! He'd had an accident. Then she flushed with guilt because she hadn't thought of Davy first. And found it was neither Jake nor the school with bad news, but Margaret Parker making a brief duty call from Florence.

When Jake arrived, right on the stroke of seven, Sarah threw open the door with a smile of such passionate welcome he took her in his arms, careless of the bag of bottles he was carrying.

'I just had a phone call,' she said breathlessly, once he'd stopped kissing her.

'Something wrong with Davy,' said Jake sharply.

'No. It was my grandmother, reporting in from Florence.' Sarah smiled sheepishly as she went ahead of him to the kitchen. 'But I was certain it was you, saying you couldn't come.'

'Why on earth should you think that?' he said, mystified, and put the bottles on the table. 'The champagne should be chilled, by the way.'

Sarah put it in the fridge, then turned to face him. 'Because I felt so happy. I was sure something had happened to spoil it.'

Jake took her hands, his eyes spearing hers. 'Sarah Tracy, I swear I will never consciously do anything to make you unhappy. Believe it.'

Sarah did believe it, and made it plain in a way Jake liked so much it was a long time before she came back to earth sufficiently to think of food. 'This won't do,' she said severely. 'Time I started dinner.'

Because Jake insisted on helping her the meal took rather longer to arrive at the table than Sarah had intended. But despite too many cooks everything turned out well. Jake was lavish with his praise, and the occasion was made even more festive by the champagne which Sarah enjoyed much more than the wine at the wedding.

'Why is that, do you think?' she said dreamily.

'Simple, my darling. We're drinking it to celebrate our engagement.' Jake grinned. 'In which case I could probably have got away with something a lot less pricey than this.'

'Cheapskate!' Sarah made a face at him. 'Though you're absolutely right.'

'But for tonight I wanted only the best.' Jake assured her.

'I did, too.' Sarah chuckled. 'Surprising though it may be, Mr Hogan, courgette flowers and fillet steaks are not part of my normal diet.'

Later they made for the sofa in the sitting room and left the curtains open so they could watch the sun set over the garden, Sarah curled up against Jake in utter contentment.

'We must make the most of this, Jake,' she said with a sigh.

He nodded. 'Tomorrow night you want free for Davy, of course, but I'll see you both on Saturday evening. How do I play that? Do I just drop you back here afterwards?'

'If she's happy you can come in for coffee.'

Jake snapped his fingers suddenly. 'Don't move. I'll be back in a second.' He went out into the hall for his jacket and came back with a square leather box. 'Go on, open it,' he said, handing it to Sarah.

She looked at him questioningly, then opened the box, her eyes like saucers when she found four rings inside.

'I knew you wouldn't want to make it official until Davy's in on it, but I was determined to put a ring on your finger tonight, Sarah,' said Jake. 'My name is good with the jeweller in the Parade. He let me bring these to see which one you preferred. Don't worry about the size. That can be adjusted.'

Sarah closed the box with a snap and climbed into his lap to kiss him. 'I love you so much, Jake Hogan.'

He shook her slightly. 'Hell, you scared me, Sarah. I thought you were going to throw the box back at me.'

For answer she kissed him with such fervour both of them forgot the rings and everything else for a while.

When Jake released her at last Sarah sat up to open the box again.

'Which one do you like best?' she asked breathlessly.

'Which, roughly translated, means which one costs least, I suppose! All four rings carry much the same price tag, which the jeweller was kind enough to remove before handing them over.' Jake grinned. 'You see? I'm getting to know you so well!'

Sarah was dazzled by all the rings. But the one she loved at first sight was a cluster of tiny diamonds set in a cushion round a raised central ruby.

'The others are modern, but that one's circa 1905—Edwardian,' said Jake, and took it from its slot to slide on Sarah's finger.

'That's the one,' she said immediately.

'Try the others on.'

'No point. I want this one.'

'Then, just like me, Sarah Tracy,' said Jake huskily, 'it's yours.'

CHAPTER ELEVEN

TO SARAH'S relief the evening with Davy was a great success. Full of excitement about going out to grown-up dinner, Davy was impatient for Jake to arrive, and when he did greeted him with an enthusiasm which delighted him. She was impressed by his car, loved eating in the Trout's garden, and chattered away to Jake during the meal as though she'd known him all her life.

When Davy was in bed later, Jake followed Sarah into the sitting room and took her in his arms, rubbing his cheek against hers.

'I'd say that that went pretty well!'

She hugged him tightly. 'Wonderfully well. Tomorrow I'll give her the news.' She drew back to look up at him. 'Unless you'd rather I waited until you tell your family.'

'I was coming to that. How soon do you think you could bear the ordeal of family Sunday lunch *chez* Hogan? I warn you now, Mother will round up all the usual suspects for the occasion, so if you can't face that just yet I can leave it a while.'

'Only until my grandmother comes back. I'd better break the news to her first, but after that any time you like. I'm looking forward to meeting them.'

'We'll take Davy along too, of course.' Jake chuckled. 'By the way, when you were making coffee just now she repeated her invitation to sports day.'

Sarah laughed. 'Something tells me it won't take her

long to get used to the idea of *you* as a stepfather.' She sobered. 'Though you'll really be her brother-in-law.'

'No one else on the planet needs to know that,' said Jake emphatically.

'True.' Sarah breathed in deeply. 'But I'm so glad *you* do. I never thought I'd find anyone I could share my secret with, Jake. Ever.'

He kissed her very gently. 'I'm grateful for the privilege. And now,' he added with regret, 'I must go. But I'll be waiting on tenterhooks tomorrow, to hear Davy's reaction to the news.'

'I'll come straight to your place from Roedale,' promised Sarah. 'Though somehow I don't think there's much to worry about.'

Sarah was right. When she broached the subject next day, straight after breakfast, Davy positively fizzed with excitement.

'Yippee! I *like* Jake. Does he like me, Mummy? Can I tell Polly? When are you going to get married? Will you wear a long white dress? Can I be bridesmaid?'

'Jake likes you very much,' said Sarah, limp with relief. 'And of course you can be bridesmaid. But we have to wait until Grandma gets back before we tell anyone.'

'OK,' said Davy, obviously happy to agree with anything. Her suntanned face glowed with satisfaction. 'I like Jake a lot,' she added, in case there was any doubt.

'More than Brian, obviously,' said Sarah dryly.

Davy gave her a scornful look. 'Jake's cool. He talks to me as if I've got a brain. I asked him to come to sports day. I hope he does.'

Sarah laughed. 'I'll tell him.'

'Ring him now!'

'Thank God,' was Jake's response when Sarah informed him of Davy's approval. 'Now I can enjoy

Sunday lunch. Though it's going to be hard to keep the news to myself.'

'Just another few days and the entire world can know,' Sarah promised him.

With Davy back in school, and Margaret Parker still away, Jake took it for granted that Sarah would spend every possible moment with him, and she rushed home every day to do her homework in record time before he arrived. He refused to let her cook, and took her out to eat or ordered something in, but, whether they spent time in Campden Road or at his flat, by mutual consent the evening always ended early, in bed.

'It won't always be like this,' said Jake one night, as they lay in each other's arms, quiet at last. 'But right now I need to make the most of every minute.'

'You mean before my grandmother gets home and Davy finishes school?' Sarah moved back a little to look into his eyes. 'Look, Jake, are you really sure about this?'

He grasped her by the shoulders. 'Loving you?' he demanded.

'No. I know you love me—'

'I should bloody well hope so by now,' he said fiercely, and kissed her hard. 'So no more doubts, woman. At the moment I tend to rush you to bed the moment I see you, which means we haven't discussed certain aspects of our future. So, as soon as my ring is officially on your finger instead of round your neck, I suggest we start thinking about somewhere to live. A house that's big enough for you, me, Davy, plus any future additions. So don't even think of backing out now, Sarah.' He smiled suddenly. 'You can't now, anyway. I've paid for the ring.'

'Then of course I won't. I love that ring.' Sarah buried her face against his shoulder. 'I love you, too, Jacob Hogan.'

'In that case,' he whispered, 'let me remove any last, lingering doubts from your mind, my darling. You belong to me. And I'm going to have you.'

'Now?'

'Now!'

When Sarah picked her grandmother up from the airport Margaret Parker received the news with deep misgiving as they drove home.

'This comes as a shock, Sarah. I've always hoped that one day you'd find someone to trust with the truth, of course, but you've only just met this man.'

'But I knew from the first that I could trust Jake,' Sarah assured her. 'And quite apart from that I like him so much, as well as being madly in love with him.' She turned steady eyes on her grandmother's set face for a moment. 'I think I deserve this. So try to be happy for me. Please.'

Margaret Parker let out a deep sigh. 'Very well, Sarah. I'll do my best. When will I have the opportunity for congratulations?'

'This evening. Jake's coming to dinner. He wanted to take us out, but I wasn't sure how you'd feel after the flight so he's having a meal sent in.'

'How kind of him,' said Margaret, thawing somewhat. 'Have you met any of the Hogan family yet?'

'Not yet. We were waiting for you to get back. Jake's just waiting for me to give the go-ahead before telling his parents. At which point,' Sarah warned, 'he says his mother will immediately gather the Hogan clan together for a celebration meal to meet the three of us.'

Margaret eyed Sarah searchingly. 'How did Davy take to the idea of Jake as a stepfather?'

'With tremendous enthusiasm. She's even invited him to sports day. Now, tell me all about Florence.'

With Jake on terrific form, and Sarah, ring prominently displayed, so obviously floating on a pink cloud, Margaret Parker unbent enough to drink a congratulatory toast in the champagne Jake had brought, but she retired to bed straight after the meal.

'Jet lag,' she explained, as she said goodnight.

'Jet lag after a two-hour flight?' said Jake, once she'd gone upstairs. 'Or does she disapprove of me?'

'Not of you, personally.' Sarah shrugged. 'She's just in a state because you know the truth. You'll have to give her time to come round. I didn't expect her to be happy about it straight away.'

He took her in his arms, rubbing his cheek against her hair. 'The important thing to me is that *you* are happy.'

'I am. Blissfully,' sighed Sarah. 'Though I hope your family shows more enthusiasm than Grandma did.'

'Of course they will. I'll tell them this weekend, to give my mother enough notice to kill the fatted calf.'

'I'm a bit nervous,' confessed Sarah.

Jake turned her face up to his, his eyes utterly serious. 'You have nothing to worry about where my family is concerned. But even in the unlikely event that they do disapprove, it won't make a shred of difference, Sarah. As long as you love me, nothing else matters.'

When Jake arrived on the Friday evening Davy rushed to open the door to him, and told him in no uncertain terms that she was thrilled about the forthcoming wedding. Over supper Davy chattered incessantly, and was almost as downcast as Sarah when she heard Jake was away next day.

'But it's Saturday. I hoped you'd go swimming with us, Jake,' she said, disappointed.

'I'd much rather do that than talk boring old business in Birmingham,' he assured her. 'The people I need to see are only available tomorrow, unfortunately.' He slanted a glance at Sarah. 'Let me take you out to Sunday lunch instead.'

'Grandma always cooks that,' said Davy.

'We'll ask her to come out with us, to give her a rest. Then the following weekend you can all have Sunday lunch with *my* family,' said Jake.

It was a prospect which occupied Sarah constantly during the time away from Jake, but when he arrived to take them out for Sunday lunch, as arranged, he made a thumbs-up sign when Sarah opened the door to him, and told her that his entire family were delighted with his news.

'Liam, too,' he added.

'I'm looking forward to meeting him,' said Sarah. Which wasn't exactly true. She had qualms about meeting all the Hogans. 'Grandma thanks you for your invitation, by the way, but she's not feeling too good. Migraine.'

'I'm sorry about that. Tell her I hope she'll join us next time.'

Much to Davy's delight Jake drove her back to Roedale later, where her day was crowned by the triumph of telling Polly about the wedding.

'No problem about going back to school tonight,' said Jake, laughing as the child made a bee-line for her friends.

'She's settled in very well now—even wants to stay

on a week for summer school. They make dens in the school grounds, put on plays, go on picnics, and so on,' said Sarah on the journey back to Jake's flat. 'I'm glad Davy's spreading her wings at last.'

'Does it mean extra expense?' asked Jake. 'If so, let me pay, darling.'

She smiled at him gratefully. 'Thanks for the offer, but it's sorted already, from my nest-egg fund.'

He gave her one of his straight looks. 'When I'm her stepfather I'll consider it my prerogative to foot her bills, Sarah.'

'And so you shall. But not until we're married.' She shrugged. 'Silly, I know, but it would seem too much like tempting fate beforehand.'

'Sarah.' Jake took her in his arms as they went up in the lift. 'I know life's dealt you a tough hand to play in the past, but from now on things will be different, I promise. You have my personal guarantee.'

Sarah was happy to believe him. Other than her grand-mother's lukewarm attitude to her engagement, the only cloud left on her horizon was the prospect of meeting Jake's family. Despite Jake's assurances to the contrary, she was still convinced that the Hogans would have pre-ferred their son's bride to produce a daughter after the marriage rather than nine years beforehand.

Glad of the pink dress for the occasion, Sarah decided that new shoes would be good for her morale. The friv-olous sandals worn to the wedding wouldn't do to meet her future in-laws. A little frisson of excitement ran down her spine at the mere thought of in-laws, just the same, simply because it brought home the reality of mar-rying Jake.

As soon as Sarah finished work next day she hit the shops. An hour later, in possession of classic fawn pumps, she was on her way back to the office to collect her usual homework when her heart gave a leap of recognition as she caught sight of Jake in the familiar car he'd parked under the trees in the Parade. She hurried down the pavement, waving to attract his attention, then dropped her hand, colour draining from her face when a woman slid into the passenger seat and brought Jake's face down to hers. Rooted to the spot, Sarah stared in sick disbelief while she watched him kiss his companion with a casual familiarity which turned her stomach. Yet for the life of her she couldn't look away. When he raised his head at last he looked straight at Sarah, raised a quizzical eyebrow, gave her an outrageous wink, smiled his famous, eye-crinkling smile and drove off.

Sarah walked back to the office in a daze. She collected the mail, said her goodbyes, and started for home through a world disintegrating in jagged pieces all around her. But Sarah's numbness gave way to anguish as she thought of Davy. What possible explanation could she give Davy for changing her mind about marrying Jake? The truth was too unpalatable for herself, let alone a nine-year-old child. What a fool she'd been. And she had only herself to blame for letting it get so far. It had been her own fault, right from asking to share the bridal suite to the point where she'd literally begged Jake to make love to her.

'You look terrible. What's wrong?' demanded Margaret Parker, who was paying off a taxi when Sarah arrived home.

'The engagement's off,' said Sarah, and closed the door behind them as they went inside.

Her grandmother stared in astonishment. 'Good heavens, Sarah. Why?'

'I've just seen Jake with another woman.'

To her credit, Margaret Parker patted Sarah's shoulder in an attempt at comfort. 'Could it have been a sister, perhaps?'

'I certainly hope not, the way they were kissing.' Sarah's eyes flashed gold fire.

'Where on earth was all this going on?'

'In a car parked in full view in the Parade.'

Margaret's eyes widened incredulously. 'There must be some mistake, surely.'

'If someone else had told me I might have swallowed that. But seeing is believing. He looked straight at me after—after kissing the woman.' Sarah's teeth began to chatter. 'He—even *smiled*—at me.'

Margaret marched her granddaughter into the kitchen. 'Sit there. I'll be back in a minute.'

Too dazed with misery to wonder where her grandmother was going, Sarah sat slumped at the kitchen table until Margaret came back with a glass.

'Brandy. Drink it up.'

Sarah, rather astonished by her grandmother's concern, obeyed, spluttered as her teeth knocked at the glass, then as the taste registered tears ran down her cheeks. 'He gave me brandy when I told him my story at the hotel,' she sobbed. 'I *trusted* Jake. What a fool I was!'

Margaret handed her a tissue. 'I can't deny I disapproved when you said you'd confided in him, but after getting to know him a little I would have sworn myself that Jake Hogan could be trusted.'

Sarah blew her nose, then took a deep breath. 'It's not just for myself. I can get over it. It's Davy I'm concerned about. She likes Jake so much.' She shuddered. 'But I just can't bear the fact that he knows such personal things about me.'

'How did you come to tell him?'

'We—we made love after the wedding.' Sarah blushed to the roots of her hair. 'Because of Davy it was the first time for me, of course. So I had to explain.'

Margaret nodded bleakly. 'It had to happen one day, because you take after Anne in so many ways.'

Sarah bristled. 'What do you mean?'

'Anne was just like you, head over heels in love the moment she met your father. Because you were on the way soon afterwards they got married right away. But you arrived late, unlike Davy, so no one ever knew.'

'That must have been a relief for you,' said Sarah acidly.

'It was.' Margaret shrugged. 'I know you think it's ridiculous, but respectability has always been of prime importance to me. I care about public opinion.' She hesitated. 'But Anne couldn't help the nature she'd inherited.'

Sarah stared at her grandmother, forgetting her anger and grief for a moment. 'Are you saying that Mother took after *you*, Grandma?'

Margaret smiled wryly. 'Impossible to believe, obviously. And you're right. It was your grandfather, not me.' She braced herself. 'He was unfaithful to me almost from the first, you see. Anne never knew because he was discreet, and I took great care to keep it from her. But living a lie takes a toll. And it made me very hard on Anne when she was growing up. And you too, Sarah.'

'Heavens, Grandma,' said Sarah, frowning. 'I had no idea.'

'Perhaps you can understand, now, how desperate I felt when she told me what had happened with Anthony Barrett. I was demented at the thought of your father's grief, the reaction of my friends—' Margaret breathed in deeply, looking every year of her age for once, and more. 'None of which is any excuse for the sacrifice I demanded of you.'

Two pairs of gold-flecked eyes met each other in silence for a moment.

'It's been hard at times, but I don't regret it,' said Sarah at last.

Margaret cleared her throat rather noisily. 'So. What will you do when Jake comes for you tonight?'

'That's not going to happen!' Sarah's jaw clenched. 'He *saw* me looking at him and he didn't care a bit.'

Sarah was so sure Jake wouldn't turn up she settled down in front of her computer to tackle the pile of mail she'd brought home. Wearing glasses because her eyes were too sore for contact lenses after crying so much, she did her best to concentrate, but it was hard to compose lucid syntax when her mind was going round in circles like a demented bee, trying to find some logical explanation for what she'd seen.

Sarah was still so sure Jake wouldn't come she picked up the receiver from force of habit when the doorbell rang, then stiffened in fury when she heard his voice over the intercom.

'Hi, darling, let me in. It's eighteen long hours since I kissed you—'

'Get away from my door, Hogan!' she spat. 'Or I'll call the police.' She slammed down the receiver.

The bell rang again at once. 'Did you hear me?' she shouted through the intercom.

'For God's sake, Sarah, what the hell's *wrong*?'

Only everything, she thought bitterly, and left the receiver off the hook, steeling herself to ignore the frantic demands crackling through it. After a while it went quiet, and she put it back. With relief, she assured herself. Glad she'd persuaded her grandmother to go out as planned, Sarah tried again to concentrate, then jumped out of her skin when a hard hand dropped on her shoulder.

'What the hell was all that about?' demanded Jake, his eyes blazing as he hauled her to her feet.

'Take your hands off me,' she flung at him, and backed away as far as she could in the crowded bedroom. 'How did you get in here?'

'Through the back garden. I picked the lock on your kitchen door. I advise you to change it.' He was breathing hard, a white line round his mouth. 'And don't start on about the police again. Before I move an inch I demand to know what's wrong.'

Sarah pushed her glasses up her shiny nose, glaring at him through them. 'Oh, *please*,' she said scornfully. 'Don't come the innocent with me. You know exactly what's wrong.'

Jake stood with arms folded and legs apart, looming large in the confined space. 'Actually, I don't,' he said with menace. 'Elucidate.'

She thrust a hand through her hair, glaring at him. 'Did you actually think you could come here and take up where we left off after—after what I saw today?'

Jake stared blankly. 'What the devil are you talking about?'

Sarah clenched her hands to keep from hitting him. 'You. In a car. Snogging with some female in full view of passers-by. Including me. You *saw* me. You knew I'd seen you. But you laughed in my face.'

'It wasn't me,' he said flatly.

'I had my lenses in,' she snapped. 'I *know* it was you.' She moved to the door. 'Get out, Jake. Now. Or I will call the police.'

'Sarah, there's a simple explanation. If you'll just listen—'

'Get out of my sight!' She marched out into the hall and opened the front door.

Jake followed her, gave her a look which could have cut glass, then brushed past her and went out to his car. Sarah banged the door shut, deflated, and collapsed on her bed in angry tears. Hey, she reminded herself after a while, you don't do tears. She went into the bathroom, scowled at the Pentiles lining it, washed her face and brushed her hair, polished her glasses, then went back to work.

Due to severe lack of concentration it took longer than usual for Sarah to finish. She was in the kitchen, thinking about what, if anything, to eat for her supper, when the doorbell rang again. Breathing fire, she answered the intercom and heard Jake's voice.

'A word, please, Sarah.'

Her instinct was to tell him to get lost, but she'd calmed down enough by this time for curiosity to get the better of her. She went along the hall to open the door, then stood, wide-eyed, when she found two men on her doorstep. Both tall, both fair, dressed in jeans and white shirts, they regarded her with eyes of identical ultramarine-blue, one pair gleaming with amusement, the other steel-hard with determination.

'We'd like to come in,' said Jake at last.

Heart pounding, Sarah inclined her head regally, and stood aside for her visitors to go past. 'Come to the sitting room.'

'This is my brother, Liam,' announced Jake.

Sarah could see that for herself.

'Hello, Miss Tracy,' Liam said, in a voice so like

Jake's it made her shiver. 'I didn't realise who you were this afternoon.'

The penny dropped so abruptly Sarah threw a wild look at Jake, who nodded in grim confirmation.

'You refused to listen to explanations earlier, so I brought Liam along in the flesh to clarify things.'

'I was the one you saw today,' explained Liam. 'If you want further proof, Serena's outside in the car.'

'The girl you saw *Liam* kissing,' said Jake with emphasis.

'Oh,' said Sarah faintly, beset by several violent emotions all fighting at once for the upper hand.

'It's a common mistake,' said Liam ruefully. 'We're often mistaken for each other.'

'But now you're both together the difference is obvious.' To Sarah, anyway. Ignoring Jake, she managed an icy little smile for his brother. 'Sorry to bring you out of your way like this. If I'd known the truth beforehand it wouldn't have been necessary. Jake mentioned a brother, but forgot to say you were twins.'

CHAPTER TWELVE

'Cue to make myself scarce,' said Liam. 'Mustn't keep Serena waiting.'

'Won't you bring her in for a drink?' said Sarah politely.

Liam shook his head. 'Some other time, perhaps.' He held out his hand. 'Sarah, I'm very sorry for the mix up.'

'Not *your* fault,' she assured him, and shook his hand briefly.

'You take the car, Liam,' said Jake. 'I'll get a cab.'

'By all means go with your brother,' said Sarah, with hauteur.

'I'm staying!'

'And I'm going,' said Liam hastily. 'I'll see myself out.'

After he'd gone the silence in the room was deafening. In the end Jake was first to break it. He thrust a hand through his hair and turned away to stare into the twilight beyond the window.

'I should have told you Liam was my twin.'

'Why on earth didn't you?' she demanded.

Jake turned to look at her. 'It's caused problems before.' His mouth twisted. 'I was going to tell you before Sunday, obviously.'

'Sunday?'

'When I introduced you to my parents and my family, including Liam.'

Past tense, noted Sarah in alarm.

'Have you changed your mind about that?' she asked with care.

He met her eyes. 'No. Have you?'

She looked away. 'I bought some new shoes.'

Jake moved a little closer. 'A pity not to wear them, then.'

'And Davy would be desperately disappointed.'

'So would I,' he said huskily, and closed the space between them to take her in his arms. 'Is this allowed, or will you call the police?'

'No.' She let out a deep, shaky breath, her knees suddenly giving way as she sagged against him, and Jake picked her up and sat down with her in his lap.

'That,' he said roughly, as his arms endangered her ribs, 'was the worst couple of hours of my entire life.'

'It's been a lot longer than that since I saw Liam,' she said, shuddering. 'When I saw you—him—with another woman I was *heartbroken*!'

Jake swore with colourful violence and tipped her face up to his. 'I've had a word with my little brother about making an exhibition of himself in public places.'

'Little brother?' she said, diverted.

'Half an hour younger.' For the first time that evening Jake's smiled appeared. 'I gave him hell for fooling about with Serena in full view of passers-by.'

'Not your style at all,' agreed Sarah. 'But you can see my mistake. It was your car, Jake.'

He nodded grimly. 'Liam still brings his car down here to be serviced—won't trust London garages. After he'd dropped it off he borrowed mine for the day. Liam's also used to city anonymity. He tends to forget that we share a face well known in these parts. But I prefer to keep my love life private.' Jake bent his head and kissed her, and with a sigh of thanksgiving Sarah responded with fervour fuelled by relief.

She sat up suddenly, biting her lip as she pushed her hands through her hair.

'What now?' he demanded.

She groaned. 'It just struck me that your brother must wonder what on earth you see in me. I look such a fright!'

'Is that all?' Jake let out a snort of relief and pulled her back against him. 'Actually, my darling, I like the dishevelled look so much I could eat you.' He kissed her by way of illustration, and went on kissing her, until they were hot and breathless and in need of a great deal more than kisses. 'I suppose your grandmother's due home any time now,' said Jake, breathing hard. 'I want you like hell, darling, but in the circumstances I'd better go home while I can.'

Sarah licked the tip of her tongue round her lips, her eyes glittering with invitation. 'Take me with you?'

'Oh, God, yes,' he said fervently, and in minutes they were in Sarah's car, a few things thrown in her overnight bag and a note left for Margaret. With Jake at the wheel they arrived at his apartment building with a speed which should have had them stopped by the police. He parked the car, took Sarah by the hand and rushed her through the foyer into the lift, his hands under her shirt and his mouth on hers before the doors closed.

When they reached the flat Jake kicked the door shut behind him, dropped Sarah's bag and yanked her up on her toes against him. She gasped against his mouth as he cupped his hands around her bottom, the proof of his need hot and hard against her through two layers of denim. Their kisses grew wilder, her thighs parted involuntarily, and he lifted her against him so she could lock her legs about his hips. He held her cruelly tight against his erection and strode to the bedroom with Sarah clasped close in his arms, her head buried against his shoulder.

They collapsed together on the bed, Jake hard and heavy on top of her, and Sarah lay under him, returning his kisses feverishly, revelling in the weight and feel and aroused male scent of him. When the urge to mate grew overpowering he got to his knees on the bed and pulled her up with him, to undress her, both of them on fire with such desperate need they tore at each other's clothes with rough, impatient hands until they were naked together. And then he was over her and inside her and he gave a hoarse, visceral groan of satisfaction as Sarah's hands dug into his lean hips to draw him deep into her innermost core.

Their impassioned loving was too wild to last long, but so overwhelmingly sweet in its intensity Sarah's cheeks were wet when it was over.

'Tears?' whispered Jake, kissing them away.

'Only because I'm happy.' She gave a deep, unsteady sigh. 'It's almost worth quarrelling to make up like that.'

'Almost,' he agreed. 'But not quite. In future I vote we pass on the fight and cut straight to the good part.'

The rest of the week went by on wings. Margaret Parker, rather to Sarah's surprise, made it plain she was relieved to see her grandchild so happy again, and astonished Sarah by indicating, as delicately as she could, that she quite understood if Sarah wished to spend every night with Jake until Davy came home for the weekend.

'Actually, I don't,' said Sarah. 'But last night it was late by the time everything was sorted. We just needed more time together to recover.'

'Does Jake find my presence in the house inhibiting, by any chance?' said Margaret dryly.

Sarah grinned. 'Probably. Though going back to his place last night was my idea, not his.'

'In my day, of course, officially one had to wait until legally shackled before sharing a bed.'

'Officially?'

Margaret gave her a wry smile. 'This may come as a surprise, Sarah, but sex isn't a modern invention. It was all too popular with some in my day too.'

The following Saturday Davy had her wish and Jake joined them for a swim and lunch and a trip to the cinema. Then, because it was a beautiful evening, Sarah suggested a stroll in the park before going home.

'Just like a real family,' said Davy with satisfaction as the three of them walked through the sunlit park. 'Can I have an ice-cream?'

Sarah gave Jake an apologetic smile. 'She's a bottomless pit.'

'Which will please my mother enormously,' he said, handing over the money. 'She's been cooking for days.'

Davy thanked him, then spotted one of her schoolfriends with a dog on a lead, and asked permission to run off to talk to her.

'I'm nervous about tomorrow,' said Sarah, watching Davy with the other little girl and her family.

Jake halted and took her hand. 'Don't be, darling. Liam heartily approved, by the way.'

'Even though I had glasses on and looked a mess?'

'Right. So imagine what effect you'll have when you're all dressed up to impress.'

Sarah shook her head. 'I don't want to *impress*, Jake. Just to reassure your parents that their firstborn isn't making a great big mistake by marrying me.'

'Which I'm going to do as soon as humanly possible, whatever their verdict,' he informed her.

To round off the evening they went back to supper at Jake's flat, which Davy liked so much it was an effort to get her home afterwards.

'Are we going to live here with you, Jake?' she asked.

'Not big enough, sweetheart. Mummy and I are going to find a house with a special room in it just for you,' he said, ruffling her hair.

When they got back to Campden Road it was uphill work getting Davy to bed.

'It's a big day tomorrow,' said Sarah firmly. 'Lunch with Jake's family, then back to school. So sleep now, please.'

Jake held up his arms when she got back to the sitting room. 'Come and tell me you love me.'

'I love you,' she said promptly, and curled up against him on the sofa. 'So you haven't changed your mind about being a stepfather?'

'No.' Jake kissed her. 'I like Davy. And she obviously likes me. And I know very well that life isn't all swimming and fun, like today, and later, when she's a teenager bristling with hormones and attitude, things may get rocky now and then. But because she's a little duplicate of you in every way it's easy to think of her as mine already, Sarah.'

'Thank you, Jake.' She breathed in deeply. 'This is all so perfect I keep thinking something will go wrong.'

He tapped her cheek gently. 'That part's already happened, due to Liam. From now on it's plain sailing.'

'Is he bringing Serena tomorrow?'

'No fear. She's just an old flame. Serena was in school with us. Since then she's been married and divorced twice. Liam sees her now and then, when he's down, but he wouldn't dream of bringing her to a family get-together. That's strictly for serious relationships, like yours and mine, darling.' He smiled. 'At time of going to press Liam is firmly unattached.'

Sarah kissed him, then with regret stood up. 'I'm sorry to see you go, darling, but I need an early night so I can scintillate tomorrow.'

Jake returned the kiss, then reluctantly let her go. 'I'll come for you at twelve tomorrow. If you bring Davy's school gear I can drive you straight back to Roedale.'

'I think we'd better come home first, so she can have a bath before going back to school.'

'Probably a good idea,' Jake said, chuckling. 'You may have had enough of the Hogans by that time.'

The fateful Sunday dawned so bright and sunny Sarah gave up the idea of a formal dress and high heels. When Jake arrived he grinned when he found Sarah and Davy in identical white T-shirts Margaret had brought as presents from Florence, Davy's worn with embroidered jeans and Sarah's with the raspberry linen skirt.

'You both look gorgeous,' he said, and eyed Sarah's flat white sandals. 'What happened to the new shoes?'

Sarah smiled sheepishly. 'The heels were a bit much for a hot day like this.'

'You look nice, too, Jake,' said Davy, eyeing his pale linen trousers and blue shirt.

'Thank you, sweetheart,' he said, touched. 'I'll just say hello to your grandma, then we'll be off.'

The Hogans lived the other side of Pennington, in a house set in two acres of beautifully kept garden. When Jake turned into the drive it was already full of cars. Children could be heard shouting in the distance, and Davy looked suddenly anxious.

'Are they bigger than me?' she asked Jake as he helped her out.

'Not much. Don't worry. They won't bite.'

A man with greying fair hair came hurrying towards them, familiar blue eyes bright with welcome. 'Hello, son. Introduce me to your beautiful ladies.'

Jake put an arm round them both. 'Dad, this is Sarah Tracy and her daughter Davina. Only she prefers Davy.'

'Welcome to the family, Sarah,' said John Hogan, and to her surprise kissed her on both cheeks. 'My wife's Italian,' he explained, eyes twinkling. 'I've acquired the habit.' He turned to Davy, who was watching him expectantly. 'Am I allowed to kiss you too, pet?'

She smiled and held up her face, and after planting a kiss on her cheeks he took her hand and led the way into the house, where his wife came rushing through the hall, smoothing back her greying black hair.

'Jacob!' She clapped her hands together as she saw Davy. '*Bellissima*, how lovely to meet you.' She swept Davy into a hug, then whispered in her ear. 'Now introduce me to your *mamma*.'

'Her name is Sarah Tracy,' said Davy, reassured by the warmth of her reception.

'How do you do, Mrs Hogan?' said Sarah. 'It's very kind of you to invite us.'

She was immediately folded into a scented embrace. 'You shall call me Teresa,' said Jake's mother, kissing her warmly. 'And the little one is Davy, Jake tells me.'

'After my father, David.'

'Ah!' Teresa patted her cheek. 'I know about your parents—so sad.'

'Mamma,' said Jake hurriedly, 'are the others in the garden?'

'Can't you hear?' said his father, smiling. 'Your

mother shut them out there so she could meet Sarah first. And Davy, too,' he added, taking her hand. 'Come on, pet, let's go and find someone for you to play with.'

Sarah tensed, but Jake put a comforting arm round her as the little girl went off with his father.

'You must be so proud of her. She is so sweet,' said Teresa fondly, and turned smiling black eyes on Sarah. 'And so like her *mamma*.'

'Is Liam here yet?' asked Jake.

'No,' said his mother, with an ominous flash of eye. 'He is late.'

'He'll be here, don't worry.'

'Come,' said Teresa, taking Sarah's hand. 'I must introduce you to the rest of my family. They want so much to meet you.'

Jake's sisters, Maddalena and Paula, a handsome vivacious pair, took after their mother, both in colouring and the exuberance of their welcome as they introduced their husbands and children.

'You boys,' Paula told her sons, 'must look after Davy. She's a guest.'

'And you two, no squabbling for once,' Maddy told her daughters. 'This is a special day. Your uncle is going to marry this lovely lady, and Davy will be your new cousin.'

Sarah watched the children take charge of Davy, who, far from being dismayed by the prospect, was soon absorbed into the gang as they planned how to pass the time before the meal.

'She'll be fine,' Jake assured her, then looked round with a smile as a familiar figure came strolling from the house. 'At last, the prodigal. Now we can break out the fatted calf.'

Liam embraced his parents, then with a grin at Jake

kissed Sarah on both cheeks. 'Welcome to the family, Sarah. He's a good guy,' he whispered in her ear. 'Only don't tell him I said so.'

The meal was an exuberant affair, with everyone helping themselves from a table groaning with good food. The adults took their plates outside, where chairs of every description were set close together on the paved area outside the dining room window. The five children sat on a groundsheet on the lawn to eat theirs, Davy so obviously enjoying herself Sarah relaxed enough to eat everything Jake put on her plate as she answered questions from his sisters about her grandmother and Davy, where they were going to live, and what she was going to wear for the wedding.

'Forgive my wife's enthusiasm,' said Sam, Maddy's husband. He grinned at Sarah. 'She's been trying to get her brothers married for years.'

'I don't mind,' Sarah assured a rather heated-looking Maddy. 'I'm afraid we still need some fine tuning on the details.'

'House-hunting first,' said Jake, and took Sarah's hand. 'And as far as I'm concerned a wedding date as soon as possible.'

She smiled at him with a look of such glowing agreement Teresa Hogan clapped her hands in appreciation and urged everyone to eat more food and drink more wine.

Jake got up, taking Sarah's plate with his. 'I'll bring you some of my mother's famed ice-cream,' he promised, and went over to Davy to ask her preference.

'My parents are very pleased with Jake's fiancée,' said Liam, taking the chair next to Sarah.

'I'm glad. They're very kind.' She smiled at him, but the familiar blue eyes were very serious.

'I'm sorry for what happened the other day, Sarah.'

'You weren't to know I'd see you.'

'But anyone else passing by could have seen me and made the mistake you did.' His mouth twisted. 'In London I'm anonymous, of course. But here in Pennington the Hogan twins are well known.'

'Not to me they weren't,' she said tartly. 'If I'd known about the twin part it would have saved me a lot of grief that day.'

'And it was grief,' he said penitently. 'I could see that when Jake marched me to your door that evening. I could have kicked myself for causing him any more problems.'

Sarah would have liked to ask what he meant, but at that moment Jake came out from the house with handfuls of ice-cream cones, and the younger members of the party rushed to meet him, Davy included. He was laughing and licking his fingers as he came back to Sarah.

'Sorry. I saw to the small fry first. I'll bring some for you right away.'

'Sit down,' said Liam, jumping up. 'I'll do it.'

'You two getting on well together?' asked Jake, watching his brother walk away.

Sarah nodded. 'Liam's very fond of you.'

'Of course he is. We're twins.'

'Now he tells me,' she said dryly, and handed him some tissues. 'Mop yourself up.'

'I was rather hoping,' he whispered, 'that you'd offer to lick me clean.'

'What on earth are you saying to make Sarah blush like that?' demanded Maddy. She looked round suspiciously. 'It's very quiet. Where are the children?'

'Gone to play hide and seek in the shrubbery,' said Paula, and lay back, relaxed. 'Sheer bliss. Don't have any boys, Sarah. Little girls like Davy must be so much easier.'

'Don't you believe it,' said her sister with feeling.

'Are you two trying to frighten Sarah off?' demanded Jake wrathfully.

'Now then, girls,' said Liam, handing Sarah a crystal dish full of different kinds of ice-cream. 'I brought two spoons. You can share with her, Jake.'

Sarah had such a happy time with the Hogan family she was sorry she hadn't brought Davy's school things, as Jake had suggested, so they could stay longer.

'You will stay longer next time,' said Teresa firmly, 'when you bring your grandmother. We would so much like to meet her.'

'I like your family, Jake,' said Davy on the way back to Campden Road. 'Josh and Michael said I can go and play computer games with them some time, and Nina and Chloe asked if I can go to their house for a sleepover in the holidays, Mummy.'

'How very nice of them,' said Sarah, from the depths of the pink cloud she was occupying. 'It's been such a lovely day.'

'So you enjoyed it after all, darling,' said Jake, touching her hand fleetingly.

'I feel silly now, because I was so nervous beforehand.'

'Whereas the Hogans, *en masse*, took to you on sight,' he said simply, 'just as I said they would.'

When they got to Campden Road Margaret was sitting in the garden. She got up, smiling affectionately, when Davy shot out through the French windows to report on the wonderful time she'd had.

'My family were very sorry you didn't join us, Margaret,' said Jake, 'so no getting out of it next time.'

'I shall look forward to it,' she told him, and held out her hand. 'I've put your things ready, Davy, but you need a bath before you're fit to go back to school. No,' she added as Sarah started forward. 'You sit out here with Jake for a bit, and I'll see to Davy.'

'I think your grandmother's thawing towards me,' said Jake.

Sarah nodded. 'She's different with me these days, too. She found it hard at first, knowing that you were in on the family skeleton, but she's basically a sensible woman. She knew it had to happen some time.'

'Thank God it happened with me,' said Jake, and perched on the foot of Sarah's old steamer chair. 'Come and sit here with me.'

She slid into the chair with a sigh, smiling at him as he took her hand. 'You know, Jake, normally I never even think about it, but when I was watching Davy romping with your sister's children today, it was hard to believe I'm not really her mother.'

'But you are, in every way but biological fact,' he said quietly. 'And no one could be a better mother than you are, Sarah. Davy's a great kid. Which is all down to you.' The straight blue look gave due warning that something serious was coming next. 'Which, talking of children, brings me to an overdue apology.'

Sarah gave him a slow, comprehending smile. 'No apologies, Jake. I don't mind. In fact, I'm glad.'

Jake let out a deep breath, and kissed the hand he was holding. 'That hellish misunderstanding was the culprit. The other times I was prepared—'

'I've been meaning to ask about that,' she said, delighted when his face reddened. 'Were you that sure you'd get lucky after Nick's wedding, then?'

'Not at all,' he retorted, then grinned ruefully. 'But when you asked to share my room I didn't dare trust in my increasingly shaky will-power. Fortunately the men's room at the hotel was fully equipped. Which was just as well when the storm brought things to a head.' His eyes met hers with a look which brought matching colour to her own face. 'But by the time we got to my place after the quarrel I was so desperate to make love to you my brain stopped functioning.'

Sarah kissed him. 'So did mine.'

'You're not sorry we could be having a child, then?' he said, with such deep satisfaction she kissed him again.

'No, Jake Hogan. Not in the slightest.'

They sat together in dreamy silence for a few minutes, until Margaret coughed tactfully and came out to join them.

'Davy's ready, but not exactly fired with enthusiasm for the return to school. Which is only natural after such an exciting weekend.'

'Right,' said Jake, pulling Sarah to her feet. 'Let's go.'

Davy was waiting in the hall by her bag. 'I don't feel well,' she said mutinously.

'Too much pasta and ice-cream, maybe,' said Sarah. 'Tell you what, if your tummy's protesting you can sit by Jake in the front, and I'll take a back seat.'

Davy waved goodbye to Margaret, then brightened a little when Jake put a selection of the latest hits on the CD player. Sarah slid into the back seat with a yawn.

'Gosh, I'm sleepy,' she said, and leaned back gratefully against the leather. 'Wake me if I snore.'

Which totally failed in its aim to win a smile from

Davy, who sat hunched in her seat, apparently absorbed in the music.

Jake drove Sarah home afterwards, stayed to share a snack supper, then left early. 'You look in need of a good night's sleep, Sarah,' he said firmly. 'On our own, alas. Never mind. I shall warm my lonely bed with the thought that soon you'll be sharing it with me every night. So get some rest while you can.'

The following evening Sarah got home from work feeling rather flat, because Jake was in London for the day, and might not make it home in time to see her. She ate a quick supper, then settled down to finish off the work she'd brought home. When Jake rang during the evening, as promised, he told her he wouldn't be home until after ten.

'In that case,' said Sarah, disappointed, 'I'll have another early night and come round to your place tomorrow evening.'

'Early,' he ordered.

She smiled as she put the phone down, then put her feet up on the sofa, suddenly so tired she hadn't the energy to get ready for bed. When her phone rang again every hair rose on her spine when a crisp voice said, 'Irene Kendall here, Miss Tracy.'

'Is Davy ill, Mrs Kendall?' demanded Sarah in alarm.

'It's not that, Miss Tracy. Do you have someone with you?'

'Yes. But just tell me what's wrong—*please*!'

'I regret to tell you that Davina is missing.'

Sarah gasped. '*Missing?* How could she be? Have you searched for her?'

'Of course. She went to bed as usual, but when her house mother made the rounds just now Davina's bed was empty. Everything possible has been done to find her before I rang you, both in the school itself and the grounds, but without success. I hoped so much that she would be with you.'

'I would have rung you at once if she had been. But she's *not*,' said Sarah, her voice cracking. 'Have you called the police?'

'I wanted to make sure Davina wasn't with you. But I'll contact them at once.'

'I'll get in the car—'

'No, Miss Tracy. Please. You must stay home in case Davina contacts you. The moment I hear anything I'll ring you. Please do the same for me if—when you have any news yourself.'

'Yes, of course,' said Sarah unsteadily. Phone clasped in her clammy hand, she raced upstairs to tell her grandmother.

'Dear God,' said Margaret, white as a sheet. 'Right,' she said, pulling herself together. 'Let's not panic. We'll go downstairs and make tea.'

'I don't want any tea,' snapped Sarah, then closed her eyes in remorse. 'Sorry, sorry.'

'Brandy, then—no, maybe not, in case you need to drive.'

'Where to?' said Sarah blankly.

'To fetch Davy when they find her.'

They exchanged a long, silent look, full of dread knowledge of all the things that might happen to a lost child, then went downstairs to wait together.

'I'm afraid to ring Jake,' said Sarah, pacing up and down the sitting room. 'He's on his way back from London. If I tell him about Davy he'll probably break the sound barrier up the motorway.'

'What time is he due home?'

'About ten.'

'Ring him after that.' Margaret got up. 'I'll make that tea.'

When the phone rang at nine-thirty Sarah almost dropped it. 'Hello?' she said, her voice hoarse with hope.

'Sarah?' said Jake. 'Something's wrong. What's up?'

She told him tersely. 'But I have to hang up now, Jake, in case—'

'Right. I'll be with you as soon as I can.'

He rang off before Sarah could implore him to drive safely. Silently Margaret handed her a mug of tea.

'I feel so helpless!' Sarah began to pace, then dropped the mug with a crash when the phone rang again.

'Irene Kendall, Miss Tracy. No news, I'm afraid. The police have been here, so I'm just letting you know you'll receive a visit from them shortly. They're searching the grounds as we speak, obviously of the opinion that our search wasn't carried out efficiently.'

At any other time Sarah would have smiled at the indignation the efficient Mrs Kendall couldn't keep out of her voice. 'I'm sure it was.'

'My only consolation is that it's still light at this time of the year.'

'True,' said Sarah desolately.

'I'll ring off now, to keep your line open. Try not to worry too much, Miss Tracy.'

'Is she serious?' exploded Sarah. 'Try not to *worry*!'

'It's the kind of meaningless thing people say when there's nothing else *to* say,' said Margaret, then tensed as the doorbell rang.

'Jake did break the sound barrier,' said Sarah, and ran to open the door to him, then let out a sobbing cry of joy when she found Davy looking up at her with heart-rending doubt on her tearstained face.

'I had to come home,' she said. 'Don't be cross.'

Sarah hugged her cruelly close, then looked up to find Davy hadn't arrived alone. Alison Rogers stood a little way apart, watching them, her car waiting at the kerb.

'Alison!' cried Sarah.

'Mrs Rogers brought me home,' said Davy, knuckling tears out of her eyes.

Alison gave Sarah a sympathetic look.

'I saw Davy walking along the road into town, so I offered her a lift.' She smiled. 'I didn't have a phone with me so I brought her straight here. She's fine, Sarah, just upset.'

'Oh Alison, I can't thank you enough…'

'I'm just glad I saw her,' said Alison. 'Look, you obviously need to talk. I'll leave you in peace. See you later, Sarah. Bye-bye, Davy.'

Sarah watched with pride when Davy held out her hand to her rescuer.

'Thank you very much for bringing me home.'

'A pleasure, Davy.' Alison's eyes twinkled as she shook the small, grubby hand. 'But let's not meet again like that, please. Your poor mother must have been frantic.'

Davy gave Sarah a forlorn look. 'Were you?'

'You'll never know how much!' Sarah turned to Alison with a grateful smile. 'Thank you again.'

'My pleasure. Goodnight.'

Davina saw Margaret hovering in the hall and flew into her arms. 'I just *had* to come home, Grandma,' she sobbed. 'Before I went back on Sunday I heard Mummy saying she wasn't my mother. I've been thinking and thinking about it all the time, and I just couldn't bear it in school a minute longer. So I sneaked out after lights out, and waited for a bus. Only it didn't come, and I started walking, then a car stopped and Polly's mummy brought me home.'

Sarah felt physically sick. She closed the door, gazing at the child clasped in Margaret's arms, her mind frantically trying for an explanation Davy could cope with.

'First of all, young lady,' said Margaret firmly, meeting Sarah's eyes over Davy's untidy head. 'I think you should have a bath, and by that time we'll all be feeling a lot calmer. You gave us a dreadful fright, Davina Tracy.'

'I'd better ring Mrs Kendall,' said Sarah, pulling herself together.

Davy turned round in alarm. 'She *will* be cross with me!'

'Not when I explain,' said Sarah firmly. 'You go off and have a scrub in Grandma's bathroom while I ring her.'

Shortly afterwards Jake arrived, his face so haggard Sarah held out her arms, smiling jubilantly to reassure him.

'Davy's home! Grandma's taken her upstairs for a bath.'

'Thank God.' His hug endangered her ribs. 'What on earth happened?'

Sarah explained, then looked up at him in anguish. 'It's all my fault. She overheard when I was talking to you about not being her mother. And now I've got to find some way to explain.'

Jake led her into the kitchen. 'Make me some coffee, darling, while we think of the best way to tell her.'

Comforted by the 'we', Sarah put the kettle on, then leaned against Jake when he put his arm round her.

'You would have had to tell her one day, Sarah.'

'I know.' She looked up at him in appeal. 'Will you stay while I talk to her?'

'I'll do whatever you want,' he assured her. 'But will Davy want me around in this situation?'

'I don't know. But *I* want you.'

He kissed her swiftly. 'Then I'll stay.'

When Davy came in with Margaret her eyes lit up at the sight of Jake, obviously pleased to see him, and he swept her up in his arms.

'Next time you want to go walkabout you ring me and I'll fetch you myself, Davy Tracy,' he said with mock menace, and sat down with her on his lap.

Davy settled herself comfortably in Jake's hold, her questioning eyes on Sarah. 'Grandma said you'd explain once I was clean.'

'Right, then,' said Sarah, bracing herself.

Margaret met her eyes. 'I said you'd tell Davy who her mother was.'

The slight emphasis on the word 'mother' clarified things for Sarah. 'I was going to tell you this when you were older, Davy—'

'I'm nine,' Davy interrupted hotly. 'Not a baby.'

Sarah's eyes filled. 'No,' she said thickly, 'you're not. Thank you,' she added, when Margaret handed her some kitchen paper.

'Am I adopted, then?' blurted Davy.

'Good heavens, no, darling.'

'But if you're not my mummy who is?'

Sarah took a deep breath. 'It was your lovely granny, Davy. But she was so ill after you were born she just couldn't look after you. So she gave you to me. You were my very own baby right from the first, though I had to share you with Granny and Gramps later on, when she was better—Grandma, too.' Sarah smiled lovingly.

'You were lucky, really, because when you were little you had four people to spoil you.'

'I asked Sarah to be your mummy,' said Margaret huskily. 'Anne—your granny—was so ill, you see, and I was much too old. I thought Sarah would be the perfect mummy for you. And I was right, wasn't I?' Unaccustomed, painful tears welled in her eyes as all three of them waited with bated breath for Davy's reaction.

It seemed a very long time before Davy let out a deep sigh and slid off Jake's lap to go to Sarah. 'I didn't think I could be adopted, really, because everyone says I look just like you.'

And thank God for it, thought Sarah, weak with relief.

'Are you hungry, darling?' asked Margaret, blowing her nose. 'I could cook something.'

'I've got a better idea,' said Jake, and grinned at Margaret. 'Let's ring up for a giant pizza. Do you like pizza, Grandma?'

'I've never tasted it,' she confessed, smiling. 'But I'm sure it's delicious.'

The weeks before summer term ended at Roedale were a halcyon time for Sarah. Jake went with her to sports day and watched Davy win the sprint, and displayed his pride as openly as any father there when the winner's ribbon was pinned on her shirt. This momentous event was eclipsed only by the wedding, which took place soon afterwards, with Davy as chief bridesmaid, followed by Nina and Chloe, when Sarah walked down the aisle in the long white dress Jake had insisted on for his bride. There were so many contenders for Davy's company while her mother was away on honeymoon that in the end she spent part of it with the Rogers family and part of it with Nina and Chloe, and in between was chauffeured on regular visits to Margaret, to reassure her that Grandma wasn't lonely.

The housing situation had been solved with remarkable simplicity, and to Margaret Parker's deep approval. Her bosom friend Barbara lived alone in a large house not far from the Rogers home, and the lady was only too happy to move into the ground-floor flat in Campden Road and sell her house to Jake and Sarah.

'But we'll live in my flat while the renovations are being done,' said Jake, on the first night of their honeymoon.

Sarah looked out at the moonlight silvering the garden of the Greenacres Hotel and pinched herself hard.

'What's the matter?' he demanded as she winced.

'Just making sure I'm not dreaming.' She gave him a wry, wondering smile over her shoulder. 'You must admit it's a touch unreal. Not so long ago I was a hard-working single parent, then *wham* I fell in love with the unique and wonderful Mr Jacob Hogan.'

Jake laughed and turned her in his arms to look down into her face. 'Not unique, exactly. I'm one of a pair, remember.'

'Not to me,' said Sarah firmly. 'You, my darling husband, are one of a kind.'

Jake kissed her by way of appreciation, then kissed her again at length. 'It's getting cold,' he whispered. 'Let's go to bed.'

'It's not cold at all,' she said, laughing. 'Though I like the idea of bed. But first,' she added, 'there's something I've been meaning to ask you.'

'Ask away.'

'When you took us home to your parents the first time

Liam apologised for the infamous car incident, and said he'd caused you enough trouble already. What did he mean?'

Jake gave her a wry smile. 'You remember I told you that my London lady met someone else she preferred?'

'Vividly.' Sarah reached up and kissed him. 'Though I don't understand how she could!'

'Thank you, my darling.' He kissed her back. 'But I introduced her to Liam one weekend.'

'What happened?'

'She forsook me for my identical twin.'

'*What?* The woman has no taste. Besides, you and Liam aren't really identical.' Sarah smiled up at him. 'To me, darling, you're unique.'

'Definitely time for bed,' said Jake, and picked her up.

'Will making love be different now we're married?' asked Sarah, when he laid her on the wide white bed that had filled her with such misgiving the first time she'd seen it.

'Probably,' said Jake, his eyes gleaming with anticipation. 'I've never made love to a married woman before.'

'Same here with a married man.'

'Or any other man at all,' said her husband, with deep satisfaction.

'True.' Sarah gave him a glowing smile and held up her arms. 'Only you, Jake Hogan. Only you.'

Modern Romance™
...seduction and
passion guaranteed

Tender Romance™
...love affairs that
last a lifetime

Sensual Romance™
...sassy, sexy and
seductive

Blaze
...sultry days and
steamy nights

Medical Romance™
...medical drama on
the pulse

Historical Romance™
...rich, vivid and
passionate

27 new titles every month.

*With all kinds of Romance for
every kind of mood...*

MILLS & BOON®

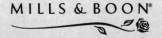

MB1

MILLS & BOON®

Modern Romance™

HOT PURSUIT *by Anne Mather*

Sara was beautiful, secretive and haunted. Matt Seton
was intrigued. He could tell she was running from
something, and common sense warned him not to get
involved – but as the atmosphere became erotically
charged he knew he couldn't let her go...

WIFE: BOUGHT AND PAID FOR *by Jacqueline Baird*

Penny is stuck: her ex-boyfriend Solo Maffeiano owns
half her home, yet she needs to pay off a barrage of
debts left by her father. She has no choice but to agree
to Solo's offer: he will pay the debts and restore the
dilapidated mansion – if Penny becomes his wife! And
he wants a wife in *every* sense of the word...

THE FORCED MARRIAGE *by Sara Craven*

Powerful Italian Marco Valante was used to taking what
he wanted – and he wouldn't let a little thing like
Flora's engagement stand in the way! Flora had been
trying to convince herself she was happy with her fiancé
– but her head hadn't stopped spinning since she'd met
Marco. And the sexy tycoon wasted no time in
whisking her away to his villa...

MACKENZIE'S PROMISE *by Catherine Spencer*

Life has led Mac Sullivan to promise himself two things:
never get involved with other people's problems, or
with women. But Linda Carr has begged him to find
her baby niece and he has the skills to help her. And
what about the prospect of an emotional search in the
company of a beautiful woman he's wanted since the
moment he laid eyes on her?

On sale 1st November 2002

*Available at most branches of WH Smith,
Tesco, Martins, Borders, Eason, Sainsbury's
and all good paperback bookshops.*

1002/01a

MILLS & BOON®

Modern Romance™

THE MILLIONAIRE'S REVENGE by Cathy Williams

Years ago Laura had been passionately involved with Gabriel Greppi. But he'd shocked her with a proposal of marriage and she'd turned him down. Gabriel has never forgiven her, and now he's a millionaire while Laura is on the verge of bankruptcy. He plans to seduce her and then reject her – as she rejected him. But will it be so easy…?

STAND-IN MISTRESS by Lee Wilkinson

Brad Lancing may be a successful businessman, but he has a bad reputation when it comes to women. Joanne Winslow is determined that her sister will not become just another notch on Brad's bedpost – even if it means she'll have to become his mistress herself!

THE MEDITERRANEAN TYCOON by Margaret Mayo

Peta is struggling to juggle single motherhood with the demands of her new boss, Andreas Papadakis. And then the Greek tycoon makes a surprising offer. He needs a live-in childminder, and for the sake of her own son Peta is tempted to accept. She takes a chance on living with the boss – only to realise there's more on his mind than a professional relationship…

THE MATCHMAKER'S MISTAKE by Jane Sullivan

When future psychologist Liz Prescott meets Mark McAlister she decides he's presenting her with the perfect opportunity to practise her matchmaking skills. Once his transformation is complete he can have any woman he wants! But as Liz sees the alpha male emerge from beneath Mark's reserved exterior she has to admit she wants him for herself…

On sale 1st November 2002

Available at most branches of WH Smith, Tesco, Martins, Borders, Eason, Sainsbury's and all good paperback bookshops.

1002/01b

MILLS & BOON

Winter
weddings

Three brand new Christmas novels

Penny Jordan   Gail Whitiker   Judy Christenberry

Published 18th October 2002

Available at most branches of WH Smith,
Tesco, Martins, Borders, Eason, Sainsbury's
and all good paperback bookshops.   1102/59/SH39

2 FREE

books and a surprise gift!

We would like to take this opportunity to thank you for reading this Mills & Boon® book by offering you the chance to take TWO more specially selected titles from the Modern Romance™ series absolutely FREE! We're also making this offer to introduce you to the benefits of the Reader Service™—

- ★ FREE home delivery
- ★ FREE gifts and competitions
- ★ FREE monthly Newsletter
- ★ Exclusive Reader Service discount
- ★ Books available before they're in the shops

Accepting these FREE books and gift places you under no obligation to buy, you may cancel at any time, even after receiving your free shipment. Simply complete your details below and return the entire page to the address below. *You don't even need a stamp!*

YES! Please send me 2 free Modern Romance books and a surprise gift. I understand that unless you hear from me, I will receive 4 superb new titles every month for just £2.55 each, postage and packing free. I am under no obligation to purchase any books and may cancel my subscription at any time. The free books and gift will be mine to keep in any case.

P2ZEA

Ms/Mrs/Miss/Mr ....Initials....................................
                                                           BLOCK CAPITALS PLEASE
Surname ....
Address ....

....
....Postcode..............................

Send this whole page to:
UK: FREEPOST CN81, Croydon, CR9 3WZ
EIRE: PO Box 4546, Kilcock, County Kildare (stamp required)

Offer valid in UK and Eire only and not available to current Reader Service subscribers to this series. We reserve the right to refuse an application and applicants must be aged 18 years or over. Only one application per household. Terms and prices subject to change without notice. Offer expires 31st January 2003. As a result of this application, you may receive offers from Harlequin Mills & Boon and other carefully selected companies. If you would prefer not to share in this opportunity please write to The Data Manager at the address above.

Mills & Boon® is a registered trademark owned by Harlequin Mills & Boon Limited.
Modern Romance™ is being used as a trademark.

valdinguer [valdɛ̃ge] vi to go flying; **envoyer valdinguer qn/qch** to send sb/sth flying

valise [valiz] nf (a) **valises** (poches sous les yeux) bags (under one's eyes) (b) Can sucker, mug

valoche [valɔʃ] nf (a) (valise) suitcase□, case□ (b) **valoches** (poches sous les yeux) bags (under one's eyes)

valse [vals] nf (a) (correction) hammering, thrashing; **foutre une valse à qn** to give sb a hammering or a thrashing (b) (cocktail) = drink consisting of beer with a dash of mint-flavoured syrup

valser [valse] vi (a) (perdre l'équilibre) **il est allé valser contre la porte** he went flying into the door; **envoyer valser qch** to send sth flying; **envoyer valser qn** (l'éconduire) to send sb packing, to show sb the door; (pousser) to send sb flying (b) (abandonner) **j'ai envie de tout envoyer valser!** I feel like packing it all in or Br jacking it all in or Am chucking everything!

valseur [valsœr] nm (postérieur) butt, Br bum, Am fanny

valseuses [!] [valsøz] nfpl (testicules) balls, nuts, Br bollocks

ⓘ This word became popular after the success of Bertrand Blier's 1974 film Les Valseuses, which told the story of two young dropouts, one of whom was played by Gérard Depardieu.

knackered, shattered, Am beat

vanner [vane] vt (se moquer de) to make digs at, Am to zing

vapes [vap] nfpl **être dans les vapes** to be out of it or in a daze; **tomber dans les vapes** to pass out□, to keel over

variétoche [varjetɔʃ] nf middle-of-the-road music, MOR

vaser [vɑze] v imp to pour with rain, Br to bucket down, to chuck it down

vaseux, -euse [vɑzø, -øz], **vasouillard, -e** [vɑzujar, -ard] adj (a) (mauvais) **plaisanterie/excuse vaseuse** feeble or pathetic joke/excuse; **raisonnement vaseux** woolly or Br dodgy reasoning (b) (mal en point) under the weather, out of sorts, Br off-colour

vasouiller [vɑzuje] vi to flounder

vautrer [votre] **se vautrer** vpr (tomber) to go flying

va-vite [vavit] nm Can **avoir le va-vite** to have the runs or the trots

veau, -x [vo] nm (véhicule poussif) = hairdrier on wheels

vécés [vese] nmpl Br loo, Am john

veille [vɛj] nf **c'est pas demain la veille** that's not going to happen in a hurry; **c'est pas demain la veille qu'ils te proposeront un boulot** they're not going to be offering you a job in a hurry

veilleuse [vɛjøz] nf **la mettre en veilleuse** to shut up, to put a sock in it

veinard, -e [vɛnar, -ard] **1** adj lucky□, Br jammy
2 nm,f lucky or Br jammy devil

veine [vɛn] nf (chance) luck□; **avoir de la veine** to be lucky□ or Br jammy
▸ see also **cocu**

arque dé-
, dig, jibe,
vannes à
to zing sb
ack

orn out, Br

(homme
Am son-
ally, Br dead,
m en verrat a

vulgar one.

dique que la traduction n'est pas argotique.

Slang sleuth

Verlan

Verlan is the most frequently used form of slang among young French people, particularly in the impoverished areas of large cities. It is formed by inverting the syllables of the word and making any spelling changes necessary to aid pronunciation. The word "verlan" is itself the inverted form of "l'envers" meaning "the other way round". Some verlan terms have passed into spoken French generally and are used or understood by a great many speakers, eg **laisse béton** (laisse tomber) – popularized by the singer Renaud many years ago – **ripou** (pourri) and **meuf** (femme). It is, however, an extremely generative form of slang and any word can, in theory, be "verlanized". Some examples: "pétard" becomes **tarpé**, "bizarre" becomes **zarbi**, and "pute" becomes **teupu** which is then shortened to **teup**. Monosyllabic words can also be "verlanized", eg "chaud" becomes **auch**; an "e" is frequently added to aid pronunciation, eg "flic" becomes **keufli** which is shortened to **keuf**, "mère" becomes **reumé** which is in turn shortened to **reum**. A term may even be "verlanized" twice – the term **rebeu**, for example, comes from the verlan for "Arabe" – **beur** – which is then "re-verlanized" to give **rebeu**. See also the panel at **L'argot des banlieues**, p.219.

---

vélo [velo] nm **avoir un petit vélo dans la tête** to be off one's rocker, to be not all there, to have a screw loose ▸ see also **grand-mère**

vénère [venɛr] Cités **1** adj (verlan **énervé**) Br wound up, Am ticked off

2 vt (verlan **énerver**) **vénère qn** to bug sb, Br to wind sb up, to do sb's head in, Am to tick sb off

vent [vɑ̃] nm (a) **avoir du vent dans les voiles** to be three sheets to the wind (b) **du vent!** clear off!, buzz off!, get lost! (c) **se prendre un vent** (être rejeté) to get turned down□, Br to get a knockback (d) **je me suis pris un vent, je lui ai parlé pendant un bon quart d'heure et** elle a rien écouté it was like talking to a brick wall, I was talking to her for a good quarter of an hour and she didn't listen to a word I was saying...

ventre [vɑ̃tr] nm **en avoir dans le ventre, avoir quelque chose dans le ventre** to have guts; **ne rien avoir dans le ventre** to be gutless

verni, -e [vɛrni] adj (qui a de la chance) lucky□, Br jammy

vérole [verɔl] nf (a) (syphilis) **la vérole** the pox (b) **quelle vérole** what a pain!

verrat [!] [vɛra] **1** nm Can (méprisable) swine, basta[rd], son-of-a-bitch; **en verrat** re[...] Am real; **un beau f**[...]

The symbol [!] denotes a very familiar term, [!!] a[...]

damn *or Br* bloody good film

  2 *exclam* **(maudit) verrat!** shit!, *Br* bloody hell!

vesse [vɛs] *nf* silent but deadly fart

veste [vɛst] *nf* **(se) prendre une veste** *(échouer)* to come unstuck; *(être rejeté)* to get turned down□, *Br* to get a knockback

véto [veto] *nm* *(abbr* **vétérinaire)** vet□

veuve [vœv] *nf Hum* **la veuve Poignet** masturbation□; **fréquenter la veuve Poignet** to bang *or Br* bash the bishop, to beat one's meat

viande [vjɑ̃d] *nf* *(corps humain)* **amène** *ou* **aboule ta viande!** get your butt *or* carcass over here!; **il y a de la viande soûle dans les rues** the streets are full of drunken bodies, it's drunken carnage in the streets; **de la viande froide** *(un cadavre)* a stiff; *(des cadavres)* stiffs

viander [vjɑ̃de] **se viander** *vpr* to get smashed up

vibure [vibyr] *nf* **à toute vibure** at full speed, at top speed

vicelard, -e [vislar, -ard] **1** *adj* **(a)** *(retors)* crafty, sneaky **(b)** *(lubrique)* dirty, *Br* pervy

  2 *nm,f* **(a)** *(personne retorse)* crafty *or* sneaky person **(b)** *(personne lubrique)* pervert□, *Br* perv; **un vieux vicelard** a dirty old man

vidé, -e [vide] *adj* *(épuisé)* wiped out, *Br* shattered, done in, *Am* pooped, beat

vider [vide] *vt* **(a)** *(expulser, licencier)* **vider qn** to throw sb out (on his ear), *Br* to turf sb out, *Am* to eighty-six sb **(b)** *(épuiser)* to wipe out, to wear out, *Br* to do in ▸ *see also* **burettes, burnes**

videur [vidœr] *nm* bouncer

vieille [vjɛj] *nf* *(mère)* old lady, *Br* old dear

vieux [vjø] *nm* **(a)** *(père)* old man; **mes** *ou* **les vieux** my folks, *Br* my old dears, *Am* my rents, my olds **(b)** *(terme d'adresse)* pal, *Br* mate, *Am* buddy; **comment ça va, vieux?** how are you doing, pal *or Br* mate *or Am* buddy?

vinaigre [vinɛgr] *nm* **(a)** **faire vinaigre** to get a move on, to get one's skates on, *Am* to get it in gear **(b)** **tourner au vinaigre** *(discussion, relation)* to turn sour; *(opération, expédition)* to go wrong□, to screw up, *Br* to cock up ▸ *see also* **vacciné**

vinasse [vinas] *nf* cheap wine□, *Br* plonk

vingt-deux [vɛ̃ddø] *exclam* *(attention)* watch out!, watch it!

vioc [vjɔk] = **vioque**

violon [vjɔlɔ̃] *nm* *(prison)* slammer, clink, *Br* nick, *Am* pokey; **il s'est retrouvé au violon** he wound up in the slammer *or* clink *or Br* nick *or Am* pokey ▸ *see also* **pisser**

vioque [vjɔk] **1** *adj* old□

  2 *nmf* old fossil, *Br* wrinkly, *Am* geezer; **mes** *ou* **les vioques** *Br* my old dears, *Am* my rents, my olds

virer [vire] **1** *vt* *(congédier)* to chuck out, to kick out

  2 *vi* *(devenir)* **virer homo** to turn gay; **virer voyou** to turn into a thug *or Br* a yob□ ▸ *see also* **cuti**

virolo [virɔlo] *nm* bend□ *(in road)*; **il a pris le virolo à fond la caisse** he took the bend at top speed

vis [vis] *nf* **serrer la vis à qn** *(sévir)* to crack down on sb, to tighten the screws on sb; *(être strict)* to be hard on sb

viser [vize] *vt* *(regarder)* to check out, *Am* to scope; **vise un peu la gonzesse!** check out that chick *or Br* bird!

Le symbole □ indique que la traduction n'est pas argotique.

Spotlight on:

La violence

Violence-related slang originates both in the speech of
the criminal underworld, popularized by detective novels
and films, and in everyday colloquial language, although
it is worth noting that the latter has often borrowed from the
former. Slang equivalents of "to kill" include the euphemisms
descendre, **butter**, **refroidir**, **dessouder** and **dézinguer**.
Flinguer is the most common term to mean "to shoot dead"
and **suriner** means "to stab to death" (from **surin** = knife).
Also found are **faire la peau à quelqu'un** and **régler son compte à
quelqu'un**. Several expressions meaning "to hit" or "to beat up" use
the same image, with slight variations each time: **casser la gueule**,
péter la gueule, or, more humorously, **abîmer le portrait** (rather old-
fashioned now) and **faire une tête au carré**. **Tabasser**, from the expression **passer à tabac**, is a very common expression. Less frequently
encountered are **escagasser** (used in the South of France), **maraver** (a
Romany term now reclaimed by the young people of the "cités") and
the ironic term **arranger** (now dated). A fight is most commonly called
castagne (the verb **se castagner** is also commonly used) and **baston**,
an obsolete form of the word **bâton** which has resurfaced to become
popular in contemporary slang (note, too, the verb **se bastonner**). A
more dated term is **rififi**, which is highly evocative of the films noirs of
the 1950s and 1960s, such as the 1955 film *Du rififi chez les hommes*.
Colourful terms used to mean "a blow" often come from words suggestive of either the fist or a projectile. The most common examples
are **chataîgne**, **marron**, **prune**, **pruneau**, **patate**, **pain**, **gnon** (from
"oignon"). Other examples include **beigne**, **taloche**, **râclée**, **tor-
gnole** and **mandale**. Someone who is about to be attacked is said to
be going to **déguster** or **morfler**.

---

vissé, -e [vise] *adj* **être bien vissé**
(de bonne humeur) to be in a good
mood; **être mal vissé** *(de mauvaise
humeur)* to be in a foul mood

vite [vit] *adv* **vite fait** quickly[□];
boire un coup vite fait to have a quick
drink; **faire qch vite fait bien fait**
to do sth in next to no time; **à très**

vite! see you in a bit!

vitriol [vitrijɔl] *nm (mauvais vin)*
cheap wine[□], *Br* plonk; *(mauvais al-
cool)* gutrot

v'là [vla] *prep* **et juste à ce mo-
ment-là, v'là t-y pas qu'il se met à
pleuvoir!** and just then, would you
believe it, it starts raining!

The symbol [!] denotes a very familiar term, [!!] a vulgar one.

voile [vwal] *nf* (**a**) **être** *ou* **marcher à voile et à vapeur** to swing both ways, to bat for both teams *or* sides, to be AC/DC (**b**) **mettre les voiles** to get going, to make tracks ▸ *see also* **vent**

voir [vwar] *vt* (**a**) **va te faire voir (chez les Grecs)! [!]** go to hell!, *Br* bugger off!, piss off! (**b**) **en voir (de toutes les couleurs)** to go through hell, to have a hellish time of it; **en faire voir (de toutes les couleurs) à qn** to make sb's life a misery, to put sb through hell (**c**) **j'en ai jamais vu la couleur** I haven't seen hide nor hair of it

vol [vɔl] *nm Hum* **elle a pas mal d'heures de vol** she's no spring chicken

volaille [vɔlaj] *nf* **la volaille** the pigs, *Br* the filth

volée [vɔle] *nf (correction)* thrashing, hammering; **flanquer une volée à qn** to thrash *or* hammer sb; **recevoir une volée** to get thrashed *or* hammered

voleuse [vɔløz] *nf Hum* **voleuse de santé** nympho, *Br* goer

vouloir [vulwar] *vt* (**a**) **en vouloir** *(être ambitieux)* to want to make it, to be keen to get to the top (**b**) **je veux!** absolutely!, you bet!, *Br* too right!

voyage [vwajaʒ] *nm* (**a**) **être en voyage** *(être en prison)* to be inside *or* behind bars (**b**) *Ironic* **si il vient se plaindre à moi, il va pas être déçu du voyage!** if he comes complaining to me, he'll wish he hadn't bothered!

vrille [vrij] *nf* **partir en vrille** to go down the tubes *or* pan

vu [vy] *adj* **vu?, c'est vu?** OK?, all right?, got it? ▸ *see also* **embrouiller**

vue [vy] **1** *nf* **en mettre plein la vue à qn** to knock sb dead, to blow sb away
2 *nfpl Can* **les vues** *(le cinéma) Br* the pictures, the flicks, *Am* the movies□; **aller aux (petites) vues** to go to the *Br* pictures *or* flicks *or Am* movies□ ▸ *see also* **air**

vulgos [vylgos] *adj* vulgar□, coarse□

WXYZ

wakos [wakos] *nm* (*abbr* **Walk-man®**) Walkman®□

witz [vits] *nm* Suisse (*plaisanterie*) joke□

WW [dubləvedubləve] *adj inv* brand new□

ⓘ In France new cars are given temporary registration plates marked with the letters WW until full registration has taken place.

X [iks, ɛks] *nf* (*ecstasy*) X, E

yaourt [jaurt] *nm* (*charabia*) = type of gibberish which imitates English sounds without forming actual words, used by people who want to sound as if they are talking or singing in English ▸ *see also* **pédaler**

yecs [jɛks] *nfpl* Cités (*verlan* **couilles**) balls, nuts, *Br* bollocks

yeux [jø] *nmpl* **avoir les yeux qui se croisent les bras** to be cross-eyed□; **coûter les yeux de la tête** to cost a fortune *or* a bundle *or Br* a packet; **il n'a pas les yeux en face des trous** (*il est mal réveillé*) he hasn't come to yet, his brain isn't in gear yet; (*il n'est pas observateur*) he's as blind as a bat, he never sees what's going on right in front of him; **il a une petite amie/une bagnole, attention les yeux!** you should see his girlfriend/car!, his girlfriend/car is an absolute honey *or Br* cracker!; **il n'a pas froid aux yeux** he's got plenty of nerve, he's not backward in coming forward; **il/ça me sort par les yeux** I can't stand *or Br* stick him/it; **il a les yeux plus grands que le ventre** (*il est trop gourmand*) his eyes are bigger than his belly *or* his stomach; (*il est trop ambitieux*) he's bitten off more than he can chew ▸ *see also* **crever, merde, merlan, œil, poche**

yo [jo] *exclam* yeah!

youde [jud] Offensive **1** *adj* Jewish□, yid

 2 *nmf* yid, kike, *Am* hebe

yougo [jugo] Formerly Offensive **1** *adj* (*abbr* **yougoslave**) Yugoslav□, Yugoslavian□

 2 *nmf* **Yougo** (*abbr* **Yougoslave**) Yugoslav□, Yugoslavian□

youpin, -e [jupɛ̃, -in] Offensive **1** *adj* Jewish□, yid

 2 *nm,f* yid, kike, *Am* hebe

youtre [jutr] Offensive **1** *adj* Jewish□, yid

 2 *nmf* yid, kike, *Am* hebe

youve [juv], **youvoi** [juvwa] *nm* (*verlan* **voyou**) hooligan□, *Br* yob, chav, *Am* hood

yoyoter [jɔjɔte] *vi* (**a**) (*mal fonctionner*) to be playing up, *Br* to be on the blink, *Am* to be on the fritz (**b**) (*déraisonner*) to be off one's head *or* rocker, to have a screw loose

yvette [ivɛt] *nf Can Pej* housewife□, homemaker□

zapper [zape] **1** *vt* (**a**) *(supprimer)* to scrap, to scratch (**b**) *(oublier)* to forget□; **excuse-moi, mais j'ai complètement zappé** sorry, I completely forgot *or* it totally slipped my mind (**c**) *(négliger)* to neglect□; **je l'ai un peu zappé ces derniers temps** I've been neglecting him a bit lately
  2 *vi (changer de chaîne)* to channel-surf, to channel-hop

zappette [zapɛt] *nf* remote control□, zapper

zarbi [zaʁbi] *adj (verlan* **bizarre**) strange□, weird□, freaky

zarma [zaʁma] *exclam* God!, *Br* blimey!, *Am* gee (whiz)!

zen [zɛn] *adj inv* **être/rester zen** to be/stay cool

zeph [zɛf] *nm (abbr* **zéphyr**) wind□

zéro [zeʁo] **1** *adv* **il est bien gentil, mais pour le travail, zéro!** he's nice enough, but when it comes to work he's a dead loss
  2 *nm* (**a**) *(individu nul)* nonentity□, nobody□, zero (**b**) **les avoir à zéro** to be scared stiff *or* witless ▶ *see also* **boule, trouillomètre**

zézette [zezɛt] *nf (sexe de l'homme)* willy, *Am* peter, johnson; *(sexe de la femme)* pussy, *Br* fanny

zgueg [!] [zgɛg] *nm* dick, cock, prick

ziav [zjav] *exclam (verlan* **vas-y**) stop it!, get out of here!

zicmu [zikmy] *nf (verlan* **musique**) music□, sounds, tunes

zieuter [zjøte] *vt* to check out, to eyeball, *Am* to scope

zieverer [zivəʁe] *vi Belg* to talk drivel *or Br* rubbish

zig [zig] *nm* guy, *Br* bloke

zigomar [zigɔmaʁ], **zigoto** [zigɔto] *nm* crackpot, crank, *Am* kook; **faire le zigoto** to act the fool, to clown around

zigouigoui [zigwigwi] *nm Hum* (**a**) *(pénis)* willy, *Am* peter, johnson (**b**) *(sexe de la femme)* pussy, *Br* fanny (**c**) *(objet)* thingy, whatsit

zigouiller [ziguje] *vt* to bump off, to liquidate, to ice

zigoune [zigun] *nf Can* roll-up, rollie, rolly

zigue [zig] = **zig**

zig-zig [zigzig] *nm* **faire zig-zig** to have a bit of nookie *or Br* rumpy-pumpy, *Am* to get jiggy with it

zinc [zɛ̃k] *nm* (**a**) *(comptoir de café)* bar□ (**b**) *(avion)* plane

zinzin [zɛ̃zɛ̃] *adj* loopy, *Br* barmy, *Am* loony-tunes

zique [zik] *nf* music□, sounds, tunes

ziva [ziva] *(verlan* **vas-y**) **1** *exclam* no way!, get out of here! **ziva! je l'invite pas à ma teuf, ce gros nul!** no way! *or* get out of here!, I'm not inviting that loser to my party!
  2 *nmf (personne) Br* chav, pikey, *Am* trailer trash

zizi [zizi] *nm* (**a**) *(pénis)* willy, *Am* peter, johnson (**b**) *(sexe de la femme)* pussy, *Br* fanny (**c**) **faire zizi panpan** to have a bit of nookie *or Br* rumpy-pumpy, *Am* to get jiggy with it

zizique [zizik] *nf* music□, sounds, tunes

zob [!] [zɔb] *nm* dick, cock, *Br* knob

zomblou [zɔ̃blu] *nm (verlan* **blouson**) jacket□

Le symbole □ indique que la traduction n'est pas argotique.

zonard, -e [zonar, -ard] *nm,f (marginal)* dropout

zone [zon] **1** *adj (sans intérêt, de mauvaise qualité)* crap, lousy

2 *nf* (**a**) **la zone** *(banlieue misérable)* the rough area□, *Br* the dodgy part of town, *Am* the hood; *(endroit pauvre)* dump, hole, dive; *(endroit sale)* tip, pigsty, bombsite (**b**) **c'est la zone!** it sucks!, it's the pits!, *Am* it blows! (**c**) **se taper la zone** to feel like a total loser *or Br* a right prat

zoner [zone] **1** *vi* (**a**) *(traîner)* to hang around, to bum around (**b**) *(faire)* **qu'est-ce que tu zones?** what are you up to?

2 se zoner *vpr* to hit the sack *or* the hay *or Am* the rack

zonga [zɔ̃ga] *nm Cités (verlan* **gazon**)

(marijuana) grass, weed

zonzon [zɔ̃zɔ̃] *nf Cités* slammer, clink, *Br* nick, *Am* pen

zoulette [zulɛt] *nf Cités* chick, *Br* bird

zoulou [zulu] *nm (jeune noir)* = young black man

zozo [zozo] *nm* jerk, *Br* pillock

zwanze [zwãz] *nf Belg* joke□; **faire la zwanze** to go out and have fun□, to party; **mettre de la zwanze** to liven things up□, to get things going□

zwanzer [zwãze] *vi Belg (plaisanter)* to joke□; *(faire la fête)* to go out and have fun□, to party

zyeuter [zjøte] = **zieuter**

zyva [ziva] = **ziva**